Tricky Business

Frank and Joe hurried down the driveway. All of a sudden, they heard the motor of a truck start up behind them. They turned to see a pair of high-beam headlights flash on.

Frank and Joe raced into the Trusty parking field as the truck bore down on them.

"Scatter!" Frank shouted.

The truck swerved, first toward Frank, then toward Joe. The brothers barely had time to think. Then Frank spotted a low brick wall at the end of the parking field.

"Joe!" Frank yelled. "The wall! Just get to the wall and dive!"

The truck followed right after them, picking up speed. It screeched to a halt, circled, and came back for the kill!

The Hardy Boys Mystery Stories

Available from MINSTREL Books

The HARDY BOYS®

TRICKY BUSINESS

FRANKLIN W. DIXON

A MINSTREL® BOOK

PUBLISHED BY POCKET BOOKS

New York   London   Toronto   Sydney   Tokyo

A MINSTREL PAPERBACK *ORIGINAL*

A Minstrel Book published by
POCKET BOOKS, a division of Simon & Schuster. Inc.,
1230 Avenue of the Americas, New York N.Y. 10020

Copyright © 1988 by Simon & Schuster Inc.
Cover artwork copyright © 1988 by Paul Bachem

ISBN: 0-671-64973-6

Produced by Mega-Books of New York, Inc.

First Minstrel Books Printing January, 1988

10 9 8 7 6 5 4 3 2

THE HARDY BOYS MYSTERY STORIES, A MINSTREL BOOK
and colophon are trademarks of Simon & Schuster Inc.

THE HARDY BOYS is a registered trademark
of Simon & Schuster Inc.

Printed in the U.S.A.

Contents

TRICKY
BUSINESS

1 Night Flight

"What a great concert!" Frank Hardy said as he maneuvered the family station wagon out of the Pine Beach Civic Center parking lot.

"Iron Tiger was amazing. They're definitely better live than on their records," said his brother, Joe, "and the Blaster Boys were a perfect opening act."

"Perfect," agreed Frank.

Frank's girlfriend, Callie Shaw, chimed in, "And *you* didn't want to *come.*"

"That's because Frank was afraid that at eighteen he'd be the oldest guy at the concert," Joe's girlfriend, Iola Morton, said in a teasing voice.

"Well, what did I tell you?" Frank said with a grin. "The average age of the kids in that auditorium couldn't have been more than fourteen."

Iola stared out the window at the bumper-to-bumper traffic. "If those kids were so young, then

1

where did all these cars come from?" she demanded. "To get here, they had to *drive* here. Which means they're old enough to have licenses."

"Not necessarily," Frank shot back. "Their parents probably drove them here."

"Actually, I noticed a lot of people at the concert who looked almost old enough to be *our* parents," Callie put in.

Frank slowly inched the car forward. After a few feet, he had to stop again.

"I can't believe all this traffic," Joe said.

"I think we're going to be here all night," Callie responded with a sigh. "At this rate, we'll never get back to Bayport."

"Well, I have nothing better to do, anyway," Iola said. "I mean, if I go home, I'll just have to listen to Chet tell me *again* how *happy* he is that he joined the Trusty Teens."

All heads suddenly turned toward Iola.

"Your brother joined the Trusty Teens?" Joe said in disbelief.

"You mean he didn't tell you?" Iola opened her green eyes wide. "Then I hope he won't be mad at me for opening my mouth."

"I hear they're a high-powered bunch," Frank said. "Chet's too mellow for them."

"Wait a minute, guys. What are the Trusty Teens?" asked Callie.

"The Trusty Teens is a national sales organization that was founded in the late fifties," Frank explained. "Adults run the company, but the whole sales force is between the ages of sixteen and nineteen. After that, a salesperson can become a management trainee."

"But what do they sell?" Callie wanted to know.

"Household products and personal-care items like shampoo and cosmetics," answered Iola. "The Trusty Teens sell this stuff for the Trusty Home Products Company."

As they talked, the traffic jam let up somewhat and cars began to move at a slow but steady pace. The exit for the road to Bayport was just ahead. Frank eased the wagon into the right-hand lane of the four-lane highway.

"Chet's all excited because now he has a part-time job, and he doesn't have to worry about what he's going to do this summer," Iola told them. "The problem is, though, that he can make extra money —bonuses—by recruiting other teens and getting a percentage of their sales."

"Oh, no!" Joe said with a groan. "I hope he doesn't try to recruit *us!*"

"You can handle it," Frank said to his brother. "Anyone who's as good as you are at keeping from getting tackled out on the football field shouldn't have any problem outmaneuvering Chet."

Chet Morton was always getting involved in some new hobby or moneymaking scheme. Until now he had usually avoided any kind of organized activity, except of course for the Bayport High football team. Frank and Joe, who were Chet's teammates and best friends, watched in amused silence as he jumped from activity to activity, sometimes juggling several at the same time.

"It's a good thing Chet doesn't approach friendship the way he does hobbies," Frank commented. "Otherwise he would have gone through the entire student body at Bayport High by now."

"Give him time," Callie said, her brown eyes twinkling. "I mean, summer's just gotten started. And if the Trusty Teens is as high-powered as you say it is . . ." Before Callie could finish her sentence, a red sports car with a black roof suddenly came barreling down the shoulder of the road at top speed, nearly sideswiping the Hardys' car. It sideswiped the car in front, swerved back onto the road, and zoomed across the intersection, ignoring the red light.

"Whew!" said Joe. "Where does he think *he's* going?"

"What a maniac!" said Callie.

"Did you get a look at the driver?" Iola asked.

"Just a quick one," Frank said. "He had red hair, and I think there was a dark-haired girl next to him."

"They sure were in a big hurry," Callie said.

"Yeah," replied Joe. "In a big hurry to cause an accident!"

At the light, traffic dispersed in several directions. The congestion eased, and Frank, Joe, and the girls soon were zipping along on the parkway toward Bayport.

Joe steered Iola back to their previous conversation. "So, has Chet been bugging you to join the Trusty Teens?" he asked her.

"Well, he *has* been hinting around that he'd like me to attend one of the meetings," Iola answered. "What do they call them? Oh, right. *Saleathons.*"

She turned to Callie, "And I'm sure he wouldn't mind if I brought *you* along."

"Me?" Callie said, pretending to be shocked. "Forget it. I couldn't sell acorns to a squirrel in winter."

"Oh, I don't know about that. According to Chet, once Bob Goodrich, the local Trusty manager, gets hold of you, you're never the same."

"For better or for worse?" Frank asked.

"You'd have to judge that for yourself," Iola teased. Then she asked, "How does Chet seem to you guys these days?"

"I don't know," Frank said. "We've hardly seen him. And now I know why."

"I heard that the Trusty Teens hold these all-day rallies where they try to convince you that you should spend your whole life selling Trusty products and recruiting other salespeople," Joe said. "I just hope Chet doesn't fall for that kind of brainwashing."

"Hey, when did you ever know Chet to fall for anything?" Frank said jokingly.

Everybody laughed. Chet's schemes had been known to backfire in some pretty crazy ways, and he often had to ask the Hardys to bail him out of the situations he got himself into.

"Aren't we pretty close to the Trusty Home Products complex now?" Joe asked.

Frank nodded. "It's up ahead, on the next road we come to."

"Why don't we check it out?" Callie suggested. "I've never seen it before."

"Well, okay," agreed Frank. "But there's not much to see. It's just a big warehouse with offices and an auditorium attached to it." Frank moved over a lane in order to be ready to make the left turn onto Industrial Way. The Trusty complex was located in the industrial area of Pine Beach, on the outskirts of town.

As they neared the turnoff, the car's headlights picked up the figure of a young man sprinting across the road from the left side. He was just far enough away so that there was no real danger of hitting him, but Frank slowed down, anyway. The young man dashed into some tall weeds at the right-hand side of the road before the Hardys or the girls could get a good look at him.

"Can you believe that guy? He didn't even look to see if any cars were coming. Wonder why he was running so fast."

"If I get my hands on him," Joe said angrily, "he'll never do a stupid thing like that again, at least not in front of us!"

Frank smiled at his brother's typically hotheaded response. Frank sometimes kidded Joe, saying he should have been born with red hair instead of blond, considering what a reputation redheads have for their tempers. Then Joe would kid Frank, too, saying he was surprised his brother's dark brown hair hadn't turned gray yet from all the fatherly advice he gave him.

Frank speeded up a little and made the left turn onto Industrial Way. Ahead of them were several large buildings. From the side of one rose a big sign.

"Trusty Home Products," Joe read. "Not much to see . . ."

But even as he was speaking, a muffled roar drowned out his words. The sign tore loose from the building, and flames began to rise from the roof!

2 A Plea for Help

"Oh, no!" Iola said. "I hope my brother's dreams of riches haven't just gone up in smoke."

Joe looked at Frank and said, "Do you think that guy we saw running across the road had anything to do with this?"

"I don't know, but we can't go after him now," Frank said. "We'd better see if anyone is in that building, and if they're in danger!"

He raced the car up the long, winding driveway of the Trusty complex, stopping a safe distance from the burning building. As they scrambled out of the car, a man came running down the drive. He slowed when he came to the station wagon and flung himself, half out of breath, against the side. After taking a moment to recover, he pointed a finger in the direction of the road.

In a hoarse voice the man shouted, "He did it! He tried to kill me!".

"Hey, calm down, mister," Frank said quietly. "Who tried to kill you?"

"Quayle," the man said in a calmer voice. "Andy Quayle."

"I wonder if that's the guy we just saw," Joe said to his brother.

"Blond hair, about five-ten, slim? That's Quayle," said the man, who was himself about the same height, but of medium build. He looked to be in his early forties.

"Where did you see him?" asked the man.

"He ran across the road back there, in front of our car," said Iola.

"We really didn't get a close look at him," added Frank. "He seemed to come out of nowhere."

"Look," Callie said, pointing to the Trusty building. "I think that fire's just about out."

As she spoke, one last flame shot out of a small wing at the side of the building, and then thick smoke blanketed the air just next to it.

Frank said, "It's almost out, Mr. . . ."

"Goodrich, Bob Goodrich. I'm the executive manager of the East Coast branch of Trusty Home Products Company."

"Well, Mr. Goodrich, it doesn't look like it was much of an explosion and fire to start with," said Frank.

"It was enough to scare the living daylights out of me," Goodrich said. "I don't know about you, but

9

I'm not used to being at the scene of an explosion. It's a little wearing on the nerves."

"If you don't mind my asking," Frank said, "what do you keep in that part of the complex?"

"It's the warehouse. And we just store the usual stuff there—cleaning products and such. Nothing explosive, if that's what you're getting at. Quayle must have brought some dynamite or another kind of explosive with him. I knew he was angry at me, but I never dreamed he'd try to kill me." Goodrich paused and looked at the Hardys and the girls. "Look, who are you kids, anyway?" he asked with a frown. "And what are you doing here?"

"I'm Frank Hardy, and this is my brother, Joe, and these are our friends Callie Shaw and Iola Morton. We were just on our way back to Bayport, when—"

"Did you say Hardy, from Bayport?" interrupted Goodrich. "Seems like I know that name from somewhere, but I can't place it."

Joe said, "Our fa—" but Frank nudged him, and he didn't finish.

"What were you about to say?" Goodrich asked.

"Oh, nothing," Joe said, quickly recovering. "Just that it's not such an uncommon name."

Joe realized he had almost broken one of their rules. They had agreed that, whenever they got into a situation that might require some investigating, it was a good idea to keep a low profile at first. Blurting out that not only you but your father and

10

brother were detectives was not the thing to say to strangers.

Just then a worried-looking security guard came running up to them.

"Where have you been?" Goodrich demanded before the man could say anything. "Somebody blows up my warehouse, and you don't even stop him!"

"I—I'm sorry, Mr. Goodrich," gulped the guard. "I was making my rounds. I was on the other side of the building when it happened."

"I don't want any excuses!" Goodrich snapped. "Get out of here—now! I'm going to call that company of yours and have you fired!"

Without saying another word, the guard disappeared in the direction of the parking lot.

Suddenly, they all heard a mixture of sirens. To clear the path, Frank pulled the station wagon off the driveway into the parking area. A minute later, a police car, with lights flashing, and two fire engines raced up the long driveway.

The police car stopped, and a tall, gray-haired police officer got out. "What's going on here, Bob?" said the officer. "The fire department called the station, and I got *their* call on my radio. It's a good thing you put in that new alarm system, connected to the fire department."

"Andy Quayle, one of my salespeople, tried to blow up my warehouse," Goodrich said. "He's been acting pretty strange lately, but I never dreamed he'd go and do a thing like that."

11

Frank and Joe glanced at each other. The same question was bothering both of them: why was Goodrich so sure it was Quayle who'd set off the explosion?

Just then, the CB radio in the police car squawked. The officer hurried over to his car, reached through the window, and picked up the receiver. "Sergeant Prescott here . . . Right, Chief . . . I'm handling it . . . Yeah," said Prescott. He listened for a few more minutes, then he replaced the receiver. He walked back to the Hardys, the girls, and Goodrich.

"That was Chief Rudin. He's going on vacation tomorrow. I'm in charge until he gets back." Prescott sighed and added, "He gets the vacation and I get the hassles."

He looked up at the warehouse. Fire fighters were busy dousing the last remnants of the blaze. There was hardly any breeze, but some of the smoke had drifted down the road to where they were standing.

Prescott looked at the warehouse and shook his head. Then he turned to Goodrich. "A kid sixteen, seventeen, has to be real angry, maybe even crazy, to try to blow up a building. He could have killed somebody. What was bothering him?" he asked.

"Well, I had to fire him today. I got complaints from customers that he was taking orders and checks and not delivering items on time," replied Goodrich. "I had to try to straighten out his sales receipts, so I asked him to come see me."

12

"At this time of night?" said Prescott.

"No," Goodrich said. "He was supposed to come at eight. But he didn't show. I had so much work to do that I figured I'd just stay in case he was late. Finally, I decided to go home. I was leaving the building when I heard noises and saw Andy running from the warehouse. Then I heard the explosion.

"I was lucky not to have been killed in that explosion," Goodrich continued, "but I don't want him around to try again. Mac, please find Quayle and arrest him for attempted murder." He motioned toward Frank and Joe and the girls. "Even these kids saw him."

Sergeant Prescott eyed the Hardys, Callie, and Iola. "Is that true?"

"Not exactly, Sergeant," replied Frank. "We were driving along and a guy dashed out into the road. He was only in front of our headlights for a few seconds."

"I doubt if we'd be able to recognize him," Joe added. Iola and Callie nodded in agreement.

The sergeant hesitated. He looked annoyed at not being able to get a definite identification of Quayle from Frank, Joe, Callie, and Iola. But finally he said, "All right, Bob, I'll try to round him up. I'd like you four to stay here," he said to the others. "Sergeant Clement will be arriving shortly to take a formal statement from you." He nodded to Goodrich, then he got into his car and drove away.

13

A few minutes later one of the fire fighters came over to them. His face was blanketed with soot.

"I'm Lieutenant Garcia of the Pine Beach Fire Department," he said. He looked at Goodrich and asked, "Do you own this place?"

"No, not exactly. I'm the executive manager here. Name's Bob Goodrich."

The lieutenant wiped the perspiration off his forehead with a soot-blackened hand. "You were lucky, Mr. Goodrich. All the damage to the building was confined in that one small wing. That's new, isn't it? Having it self-contained like that with a fire door sure helped. I can't make any promises, but I doubt there's any structural damage outside of that section of the roof. And of course, whatever you stored in that room is a total loss."

Goodrich groaned.

Lieutenant Garcia continued, "My men will be finished soon. I suggest you call your insurance agent so you can get started filling out those claim forms. We'll have somebody around tomorrow to investigate."

"It was arson," Goodrich blurted out. "I'm positive that Andy Quayle, a kid I've been having some trouble with, set the fire with some explosives."

"Oh? Well, we'll be able to check all that out," said Garcia.

"Sergeant Prescott is trying to bring Quayle in now," said Goodrich.

Lieutenant Garcia stared at him. "Wait a minute. Did you say Andy Quayle?"

14

"That's right," Goodrich replied. "Why? Do you know him?"

"Andy? Sure I know him. His dad and I used to go fishing together before he died last month. Terrible loss. Left Andy and his mom alone. It's been hard on them. You say Andy set that fire? Doesn't sound like him. He's a good kid. But I must admit I haven't seen much of him since his dad died." He excused himself and went to help his men replace the enormous length of hose onto the fire truck.

Goodrich shook his head and said, "I just don't know what's gotten into that kid lately. He used to be so responsible. Then, all of a sudden he changed."

The Hardys couldn't draw any conclusions of their own from the various conversations that had just taken place. They looked at Callie and Iola, who could usually be counted on to fill in anything they might have missed, but both girls just shrugged. They had spent enough time around Frank and Joe to know a lot about how they operated. But, like Frank and Joe, Callie and Iola seemed to have drawn a blank.

"Well," Frank said finally, to break the silence left by the departing Lieutenant Garcia. "I guess that's all until Sergeant Clement gets here."

"And what am I supposed to do then?" asked Goodrich, a note of desperation creeping into his voice. "Do I just go home and wait for Quayle to blow me to bits? All Mac Prescott

15

looked like *he* was ready to do was go home and watch TV!"

Just then, another police car drove up. An officer got out of the car and gruffly addressed Goodrich.

"I'm Sergeant Clement," he said. "Sergeant Prescott sent me up here to get statements, and then I'll escort you home, Mr. Goodrich. If Quayle hasn't been picked up by then, another officer will come by to keep watch over your house tonight, if you like. And we'll station somebody here, too. Sergeant Prescott wants you to know we'll have Quayle by morning. Most of the force is out looking for him."

Frank and Joe exchanged surprised glances. Prescott was more thorough than he seemed. The brothers, Callie, and Iola made their brief statements to Sergeant Clement. Goodrich made his somewhat more detailed, more impassioned one. Then he left with the police officer.

"So, do we have a case?" Joe asked his brother as they all piled back into the station wagon.

"Well, we *are* involved, sort of," Frank replied. "But it seems to me that what Quayle needs now is a really good lawyer, not a couple of—"

"Good, really *good*, detectives," Callie interrupted with a laugh.

"You got it," Frank said, grinning.

Frank drove back down Industrial Way and made a right turn onto the parkway, heading toward Bayport. They had only gone a couple of miles when they spotted a young man by the side of the road, waving his arms frantically. Frank slowed down and pulled over into the breakdown lane.

The young man came around to the driver's side and leaned down to the open window. "Am I glad you came along," he said breathlessly. "My car broke down about five miles back, and I've been walking along here hoping somebody would stop and drive me home."

Frank craned around to get a good look at the young man. His hair looked blond, and he seemed to be a little under six feet and slender. Frank figured he was about seventeen or eighteen years old.

Joe leaned forward from the backseat and whispered, "Frank, that's *him*!"

Frank gave a slight nod. Then he said to the young man, "Look, why don't you tell me where your car is. We'll drive on ahead to the first phone and call for a tow truck. I think there's an all-night gas station at the next exit. You should probably go back and wait with your car."

"No!" the young man shouted. "No, you've got to take me with you."

Frank hesitated. He was pretty sure Joe was right. And if Andy Quayle was responsible for the explosion, he could be dangerous. Frank thought for a minute and then decided that even if Quayle *was* dangerous, he and Joe could handle him. Besides, if it really was Quayle, Frank wanted to get his side of the story.

17

"Okay," Frank said finally. "You can get in the back."

Joe began to protest, but Frank said quietly, "I know what I'm doing."

Once the young man was seated next to Joe in the backseat and the station wagon had driven off again, Frank asked, "Just where is your car stuck?"

The young man didn't answer right away. "Okay, okay," he said finally. "There's no car. I just need to get out of here."

"You're Andy Quayle, aren't you?" Frank said.

"That's right," Quayle replied in a sulky voice. "What's it to you?"

"Now, look, Andy," Frank said in a calm but commanding voice. "We heard Mr. Goodrich's side of the story. You might as well tell us yours." He added, "Lieutenant Garcia, back at the Trusty complex, said you were a good kid."

Quayle looked baffled. "What was Bill Garcia doing there? Was there a fire at Trusty?"

"You didn't know?" asked Iola.

Quayle shook his head no.

"If that was you we picked up in our headlights back on the road near the Trusty complex," Frank said, "you know what happened better than the rest of us."

"What do you mean?"

"Why were you running across the road?" Joe asked. "Most people don't go jogging through an industrial park at midnight."

18

"I—I needed to get away from Trusty and think. Running helps clear my head. Besides, I had to get home, anyway."

"You don't have a car?" asked Frank.

"No, my mother has it. She drove me over to Trusty on her way to her job. She's a checker at a twenty-four-hour supermarket. She works the night shift on Saturdays."

Frank asked, "Why did you go to see Goodrich tonight?"

"You still haven't told me what happened back there," Quayle pressed.

"There was an explosion and fire at the Trusty warehouse tonight," Joe told him.

"What?" Quayle said with alarm. "The warehouse blew up?"

"You must have heard it when you ran into the brush," said Frank.

"Well, yes and no. I thought it was just a truck backfiring, or something like that. How bad was it?"

"It was contained in a small wing. Whoever set off the explosion may have known that the rest of the place wouldn't go up. But Goodrich is convinced he was the target of a murderer."

"What were you doing at Trusty?" asked Frank.

"I don't like being given the third degree," snapped Quayle. "And I don't like what you're getting at. You think *I* caused that explosion, don't you?"

19

"Listen, Andy, we're just trying to help you," Callie said quietly. "Goodrich is convinced you did it. Right now, all we want to do is get your story."

Andy shrugged. "Well, if you must know, I made an appointment with Goodrich to warn him I suspected something fishy was going on at the warehouse."

"You went to see him at eleven o'clock?" Frank asked.

"He said he'd be busy until then," Quayle answered. "I thought it was pretty strange, but I figured, why not?"

"Goodrich told us he asked you to come at eight o'clock to talk about some problems with your sales receipts, but that you never showed," Joe stated.

"He's lying!" Quayle said hotly.

"Maybe," Joe replied. "But right now you're the police's number-one suspect."

Andy Quayle looked at Joe, his eyes filled with fear. "I didn't do it," he said in a shaking voice. "You've got to believe me. I mean, why would I want to blow up Goodrich's warehouse?"

"He fired you today, didn't he?" Iola asked.

"Well, yeah, but . . . anyway, I wasn't even in the warehouse, just the office. And I wouldn't even know where to get my hands on explosives."

"Andy, listen to me," Frank said. "The smartest thing you can do is turn yourself in. Running away isn't going to solve anything."

"What do you know about it?" Andy cried. "I

was unjustly accused of a crime once before. Someone else did it, but I was the one who was nailed." He shook his head. "Forget it. I'm not letting the police get their hands on me again. I'll take my chances out there."

Although Frank was driving along at a good speed, Quayle shouted, "Either you stop this thing and let me get out, or I'll jump out!"

Frank stepped on the brakes, and Andy Quayle flung open the door and sprang out onto the shoulder. He disappeared into a stand of trees by the roadside.

"He sure acts guilty to me," Joe said.

"I don't know about that," Frank replied slowly.

"I wonder what kind of crime he was accused of before," Callie said thoughtfully.

The four fell silent as they once again drove toward Bayport. But they had gone only another half mile when the flashing lights of a police roadblock stopped their journey.

"Now what?" Joe said.

"It may be an accident, but I've a hunch they're laying for Quayle," said Frank. He brought the wagon to a stop behind a late-model sedan. A police officer was questioning the sedan's driver.

"I think we should tell them where he is," said Joe.

"Look, Joe," Frank said. "I'm convinced Quayle will turn himself in when he's ready."

They looked out the window and saw the police officer coming toward their car.

"I think you're wrong," Joe said. "I'm going to tell them."

"Joe!" Frank said. "Don't do it!"

But Joe was already out of the car. In a few minutes, he had told the officer about their run-in with Andy Quayle and sprinted back.

Moments later, they were moving on as the officer feverishly spoke into his radio.

Frank turned around. "Are you satisfied now?" he asked his brother. "You didn't even give Andy a chance to do the right thing and turn himself in."

"*I* did the right thing." Joe sat back, his arms folded across his chest.

"I hope so," Frank said as they sped off. "But I have a bad feeling we're making a *big* mistake."

3 An Arresting Situation

The next morning, Joe was the first to break the silence between the brothers. "I still say he's guilty," he insisted as he and Frank sat down to breakfast.

"And I still say you should have given him a chance to turn himself in," Frank argued.

"Look," Joe said, "let's drop it. I don't think it mattered one way or another—the police would have gotten him, anyway. I just didn't think we should have held back information from them."

"What makes you so sure he's guilty?" Frank wanted to know.

"Oh, come on, Frank," Joe said as he munched on a slice of French toast. "He had a motive, the opportunity, and no alibi. Not only that, he's the only suspect."

"So far," Frank reminded him.

Joe looked at his brother. "Then I guess the answer to the question I asked you last night is 'yes.'"

"What question?" asked Frank, frowning.

"Do we have a case?"

Frank grinned. "Yes," he said. "We definitely have a case."

Just then, their aunt Gertrude came in from the kitchen and placed another platter of French toast in the middle of the table. Aunt Gertrude, their father's sister, lived with the family. She was totally devoted to looking after Fenton and Laura Hardy and their two sons. And that wasn't easy, because in the Hardy household it seemed as if somebody was always coming or going. Everyone admitted they couldn't manage without her.

When Frank filled in Aunt Gertrude on what had happened the night before, she shook her head and said, "You boys are the only ones I know who could go to a concert and wind up in the middle of a case of attempted murder on the way home." She added, "Except, perhaps for your father."

Frank and Joe grinned at the mention of their father. They knew that what Aunt Gertrude had said about him was true. Fenton Hardy was a former New York City police officer turned successful private investigator.

"I'm glad Mom and Dad finally decided to take that vacation," Frank said. "That last case of his was really tough." He added, "And I have a feeling our case is going to be a tough one, too."

"Do you think that Quayle boy is guilty?" Aunt Gertrude asked.

"It's hard to say," Frank replied. "There's evidence both for and against."

"I think he acted pretty suspiciously for someone who's innocent," said Joe.

Frank added, "I'd like to know if the police found him last night. I'm going to call the Pine Beach police station."

"I think you did the right thing, Joe," Aunt Gertrude said. "I'm surprised at you, Frank, for wanting to stand by and let him get away."

"It looks like I'm outvoted," Frank said.

As he rose from the table to call Pine Beach, the phone rang. Frank picked up the receiver.

"This is Sergeant Mackenzie Prescott from the Pine Beach police," the voice at the other end said. "May I speak to Frank or Joe Hardy?"

"This is Frank Hardy speaking."

"Frank, we brought Andy Quayle in last night and booked him for attempted murder, among other things. We'd like you and your brother to come down to the station and go over the details of your part in the incident. We've contacted Ms. Shaw and Ms. Morton, and they've agreed to cooperate."

Frank said he and Joe would be there soon and hung up the phone.

"They picked him up," he told Joe. Then he repeated the sergeant's request.

"Look, Joe, do me a favor," Frank said. "Don't

tell the sergeant you think Andy Quayle is guilty, okay? He's in enough trouble as it is."

"Okay, okay," replied Joe good-naturedly. "I'll be tactful and discreet."

Frank rolled his eyes. Those two words rarely, if ever, could be said to describe his brother!

The Hardys said goodbye to Aunt Gertrude and headed out the door toward their dark blue police van. The van had been given to the brothers by Chief Collig of the Bayport police after the Desert Phantom case. They liked to take their mother's old station wagon on dates, since it seated more than two, but the van was their main source of transportation.

The Pine Beach police station was an old red-brick building in the center of town, next to the town hall. "It's taken us a lot less time to get to Pine Beach this morning than it did to get back to Bayport last night!" Joe said as he stopped the van. They stepped out and saw Callie and Iola waiting for them by the police station door.

The four of them entered the building and approached the front desk. When they gave their names to the officer on duty, he directed them to the squad room. They walked down a mint green corridor until they reached a door marked Squad Room. Frank opened the door.

Several police officers sat at their desks, talking on the phone or filling out reports. A number of wanted posters, containing grainy photographs of suspected criminals, were attached to the walls and columns of the room with gummed tape. One wall contained pictures of children reported to be missing or kidnapped.

Sergeant Prescott was off to the right stuffing a manila folder into a file cabinet. He looked up as they entered.

"Well, well, if it isn't my four favorite witnesses," Prescott said. "You'll be happy to know your friend Andy Quayle is being held in a cell just down the hall."

Frank and Joe looked at each other.

"Excuse me, sir, but he's not our friend," Joe said. "We just met him last night."

"To hear him talk, you all had quite a nice little chat in your car last night."

Prescott sounded slightly nasty. Frank and Joe didn't know what to make of it. Maybe he just didn't like teenagers. The Hardys, Callie, and Iola silently followed the sergeant to the far side of the room.

Sergeant Prescott's desk was right in front of a large double window, and the sun pouring in made the Hardys and the girls blink. Sergeant Prescott sized up the situation and closed the blinds. "Better?" he said. He sounded a bit more friendly.

"Thanks," said Frank, and the others nodded.

"Why don't you pull up some chairs," Sergeant Prescott said. "Just get two more from those empty desks. Some of the guys are on vacation."

When they were all seated, the sergeant went on. "Let's go over the details of what you remember about last night. First of all, which one of you was driving?"

"I was," answered Frank.

"Okay, Frank, you were driving along at approximately eleven-ten last night when you saw Quayle run across the road near the Trusty Home Products Company warehouse. Is that right?"

"We saw *somebody* run across the road," replied Frank, "but we can't be sure it was Quayle. We didn't see where he was coming from. I only saw him when my headlights picked him up. He was already starting across the road."

"Listen, Frank, we've already placed him at Trusty, and he admitted running in front of the car."

"That's true—up to a point," Frank said. "But how can he be sure it was our car he ran in front of? We thought it might be Quayle, but we didn't get a good look at him, so he probably didn't get a good look at us. There might have been two guys running across the road."

"Are you playing games with me?" Sergeant Prescott said angrily, his face turning red.

"Sorry, Sergeant," Frank said. "I was only trying to suggest that things aren't necessarily as open and shut as they may seem."

"Why are you protecting this kid? You said you don't know him, that he's not a friend."

"That's true," said Frank.

Prescott paused and sighed. Then he said, "Well,

let's get on with the rest of the report." He reviewed the incident of the night before and typed the details and the responses of the Hardys and the girls into a computer.

When he had finished, he leaned back in his chair and said, "We have pretty strong evidence against Quayle. I'm glad we don't have much to do on this case. I'm going on vacation next week."

There was a short pause. Then Frank said, "It's probably none of our business, but would you tell us what your evidence is against Quayle?"

"It *is* none of your business," replied Prescott, "but I'll tell you, anyway. We found some explosives in the woods at the side of the road, near the spot where you saw him running." Prescott shook his head. "He's a messed-up kid. He was picked up once before for attempted robbery. Three years ago, when he was fifteen."

"But that was three years ago," Iola said.

"And he was accused, not convicted," Callie pointed out.

But Prescott just shrugged and said, "Where there's smoke, there's fire."

"Could we have a look at Quayle's statement?" Frank suddenly asked the sergeant. "And Goodrich's, too?" he added hopefully.

"What do you want those for?" Prescott asked. "We don't go around showing statements to other folks who make statements." He paused and stroked his mustache thoughtfully.

"Wait a minute," he said. "Hardy—I knew I recognized that name from somewhere. You're Fenton Hardy's kids, aren't you? Your father gave a talk here on detective work last year. He mentioned he had two sons who were chips off the old block."

Prescott suddenly lifted the receiver of his phone and pushed a button on his intercom. "Gregson," he said, "bring in Quayle."

Frank asked Prescott, "Is Sergeant Clement here?"

"No," Prescott said. "Clement doesn't come in till five. He's on the five-to-one shift. Why do you ask?"

"Don't you remember? Clement was the officer we gave our statements to last night."

"Oh, right," said Prescott.

Frank was about to ask why the sergeant had wanted to hear their story again when they suddenly heard footsteps behind them. They wheeled around to see a young officer escorting a pale, rumpled-looking Andy Quayle toward them.

"Bring that chair over and sit down, Quayle," Prescott said, motioning to another empty chair. "That's all, Gregson."

"Thanks a lot, guys, for telling the cops where they could find me," Andy muttered. "I knew I could count on you."

Frank didn't want to stir up another argument with Joe, especially in front of Prescott. So he said nothing.

Andy glared at the four of them, then said, "This

police department here has got me practically hanged already."

"Now, just cool off," Joe said to him. "If you're really innocent, you don't have anything to worry about."

"Yeah, and you probably believe in the tooth fairy, too," Andy replied bitterly.

"If you need help, we'll do what we can," Frank said. "Do you have a lawyer? Have you arranged to post bail yet?"

"What do you care?" Andy said sulkily, turning away.

"He didn't want to call anybody last night," Prescott said. "But he knows his rights."

"I didn't want to bother my mom at her job," Andy said, facing them again. "But I called her this morning, and she said she'd be here soon."

Just then, they heard an insistent woman's voice saying, "Where do you have my son? His name is Andy Quayle. Where is he?"

Everyone turned to see an attractive dark-haired woman in her forties, wearing a blue-and-green-flowered sundress and carrying a straw handbag.

"Mom, here I am," Andy called across the room.

Mrs. Quayle rushed up to her son. "Oh, Andy, are you all right?"

"I'm okay, Mom," Andy muttered.

Mrs. Quayle looked at Sergeant Prescott and said, "There must be some mistake, Sergeant. My son didn't cause that explosion. He wouldn't do a thing like that."

31

"If you'll recall, ma'am, your son *has* been in trouble before," said Prescott.

Mrs. Quayle stood very still without saying a word. Suddenly she looked at Frank and Joe and the girls. "Andy," she said, "are these some friends of yours? Were they with you last night?"

"They aren't my friends," Andy said. "They're the ones who turned me in."

"What do you mean?" asked Mrs. Quayle.

There was a moment's silence, then Joe spoke up. "I'm Joe Hardy, and this is my brother, Frank. And these are our friends, Iola Morton and Callie Shaw."

Joe continued, "We were driving home last night when we heard the explosion and saw the fire at the Trusty Home Products complex. Someone ran in front of our car, then later, Andy tried to hitch a ride with us. At a roadblock I told the police we had seen him."

Frank added swiftly, "He told us his side of the story when we met him."

Mrs. Quayle looked at them. "Then you must know he's telling the truth. Can't you help him prove it?"

"I'm sure these boys would like to do some *amateur* detective work," said Sergeant Prescott with an amused look. "But what your son really needs is a lawyer. The court will appoint one if you can't afford it. Oh, and he'll need to post bail."

"How much is bail?"

"Ten thousand dollars," Prescott said.

"Where will I get that kind of money?" Mrs. Quayle said in a desperate tone.

"Well, ma'am, in that case," Prescott said, "it looks like your son will just have to stay in jail for a while."

"Not if we can help it," Frank said. "We can get Andy out," he said to Mrs. Quayle. "A friend of our father's is a bail bondsman."

"Do you believe my son is innocent?" Mrs. Quayle asked, looking at Frank.

"I don't know," Frank answered honestly. "But either way he shouldn't have to be stuck in a jail cell."

While Frank made the phone call to the bail bondsman, the public defender came and talked to Andy. Then, a few hours later, the bondsman arranged Andy's bail, and he was released in his mother's custody. Frank and Joe and the girls had insisted on staying with Mrs. Quayle at the station after Andy was taken back to his cell. Now they were all leaving the station together.

As they walked toward the curb, an attractive dark-haired girl drove up in a red sports car with a slightly dented fender and got out. She was wearing a bright blue T-shirt that said "Trusty Teen" on it. "Hi, Andy," she said in a voice dripping with phony sweetness. "Bob told me I could find you here."

"Alison," Andy said. "What are you doing here?"

"I just came by to give you a little friendly

advice," Alison said. Her voice became suddenly deeper—and nasty. "You don't belong with Trusty, that's obvious, or else Goodrich wouldn't have fired you. But I heard he gave you three weeks to leave. If you know what's good for you, you won't stick around that long. Take my advice and leave now, or you'll be sorry. Real sorry."

4 A Different Story

With a smile and a shake of her long brown hair, Alison got back into her sports car and drove off.

"What was that all about?" Callie asked in amazement.

"I don't know," replied Andy, shaking his head.

"Who was that charmer, anyway?" Iola asked.

"Her name is Alison Rosedale. She and a guy named Vince Boggs and I have been the three top salespeople for the East Coast branch of Trusty this year. We had a rivalry going—a friendly one, I thought."

"That sounded like some sort of threat," said Iola.

Andy looked shaken. "I just don't get it," he said. "Up until a few weeks ago, everything was going fine. Now I've been fired, Goodrich is accusing me of trying to kill him, and Alison Rosedale is threatening me."

"You know, there's something familiar about her car," Callie said. "But I don't know what." She thought for a minute, then shook her head. "Forget it, I can't place it right now."

Frank spoke up. "Andy, I know you're upset with us for tipping off the cops last night. But if you let us help you, maybe we can find out what's really going on."

"Just leave me alone," muttered Andy.

"Come on, Andy, give them a chance," said Mrs. Quayle. She turned to the Hardys and the girls. "Why don't you all come home with us. Then Andy can tell you his side of the story."

"Cut it out, Mom," Andy said. "And besides, I already have. Last night, in their car."

"But there might be other things you can tell us," Frank pointed out. "Background information you wouldn't have told us last night."

Andy shrugged. He walked off toward an old white sedan parked at the curb and got in. Mrs. Quayle turned to the others and said, "Just follow me. I'll talk to Andy on the way home."

Frank's van and Iola's car followed Mrs. Quayle's aging sedan down the tree-lined streets of Pine Beach. Soon, they were driving through a neighborhood that contained small frame houses. They pulled up in front of a neat white bungalow with black shutters and a red door. A cinder driveway led to a partially visible garage.

36

Mrs. Quayle welcomed them all into a small, simply furnished living room. She smiled and said, "You know, I haven't properly introduced myself. I don't know what's happened to my manners. I'm Anita Quayle. I hope you kids can help us sort out this mess.

"Andy told me as much as I could pry out of him on the way here from the police station. But I think there's more to it. Why would Mr. Goodrich dream up such an awful accusation against Andy? They've always gotten along so well."

"That's one of the things we have to try to find out," said Frank.

"What can you do for me? You're only kids my age, not real detectives," Andy said miserably.

Frank and Joe didn't try to convince Andy by listing the many cases they had solved. Instead, all Joe said was, "What have you got to lose?"

Andy looked at Joe, then Frank. Then he gave a sigh and said, "Oh, okay. Anyway, it's cheaper than hiring a lawyer." He turned to his mother. "Mom, I didn't tell you what was going on because I didn't want you to be in any danger."

"Danger!" Mrs. Quayle said with alarm. "What kind of danger?"

"I—I'm not sure. But I have a feeling that Mr. Goodrich is in big trouble. And now he thinks he can shut me up with this phony accusation."

"Start from the beginning," said Frank.

"All right," Andy said. "To begin with, I've been with Trusty for two years, since I was sixteen. Up

37

until yesterday, everything was great. As I told you, I had worked my way up to become one of Trusty's top three sellers.

"Vince Boggs, Alison Rosedale, and I all got along fine. We had different styles, and there was room for all of us to be at the top. Vince is this scientific genius, but not your typical absentminded type. Or a nerd. He's good-looking and popular with girls. He's doing so well at Trusty because he's probably figured out by computer how to get the most profits. Word is that he wants to go away to college next year, and then he won't be around, anyway.

"Alison Rosedale is very pretty. She's a real go-getter. I think she wants a career in management, so after graduation, she'll probably stick around until she can enter the trainee program.

"Anyway, there was suddenly a falling out between Vince Boggs and Goodrich. I don't know why. Goodrich didn't try to kick Boggs out of the Trusty Teens or anything, but they've been real cool toward each other. And Boggs has hardly spoken to me, either.

"Then Alison Rosedale suddenly became more aggressive around Goodrich, and kind of rude. Goodrich seemed to be avoiding her, too.

"Then she started acting hostile toward me, like I had something to do with it. I was just doing my work, same as always. Maybe she couldn't stand the idea that Goodrich was friendlier to me than to her."

"Were you and Goodrich real tight before yesterday?" Joe asked.

"Yes," Andy said. "And even when he fired me, he was nice about it."

"Goodrich said you weren't delivering orders on time and customers were complaining," said Joe.

"That's true," admitted Andy. "I guess I just couldn't concentrate one hundred percent on doing my job after my dad died."

Callie gave Andy a sympathetic look. "That seems one hundred percent understandable to me," she said gently.

Andy sighed and said, "Anyway, I went to see him last night to warn him."

"About what?" asked Frank.

"Two weeks ago, I was picking up my products at the warehouse when I overheard two guys yelling at each other," Andy replied. "I wandered over to where I heard the voices coming from, and I saw them behind a partly opened door of the warehouse.

"One of the guys was Del Carson, who has been the foreman there for the last few months. The other guy must have been new, because I'd never seen him before. I know all the guys who work at the warehouse.

"Anyway, they caught me watching them and Carson slammed the door. He stormed over to me and yelled, 'You'd just better keep your nose out of business that doesn't concern you.' I told him I thought there might have been some kind of trouble. And he said, 'If you're looking for trouble, just keep on poking your nose into my business.'

"Then, last week, when I was at the warehouse, I saw a whole bunch of new guys working there, loading cartons into the warehouse. I figured they must be summer help. Then I noticed something really strange."

"What did you see?" Iola asked.

"I've seen guys load and unload lots of cartons around there," replied Andy. "And even though they're *supposed* to be careful, they just throw them around. But these guys were being so careful about the cartons, you'd have thought they were full of glass."

"Is that possible?" Frank asked.

"No," Andy answered, shaking his head. "Trusty doesn't sell anything like that. But what happened next was even stranger. I went to the office to pick up some forms, and I saw Carson in Goodrich's office rifling through a drawer in Goodrich's desk. He stopped when he saw me, and he made up some excuse about looking for his paycheck.

"That's when I decided to see Goodrich and tell him that I thought something funny was going on. But when I saw him last night and told him, he accused me of trying to cause trouble because I'd been fired. Then he ordered me out of his office."

"How long were you with Goodrich in his office," asked Joe.

"About half an hour," replied Andy. "From about ten-thirty to eleven o'clock." He added, "He and I were the only ones in the office. I'm positive about that. But someone could easily have been in the warehouse without our knowing it. There's a security guard at the plant, but it's an awfully big building, and there's never been any reason to expect a break-in. What I can't understand is, if someone was trying to kill or even scare Goodrich, why would he try to pin it on me?"

"Good question," Frank said. "And we're going to try to find out the answer. We'll have to work fast in case you come up for trial quickly."

"I know," Andy said. "Even the public defender said she thought the police had a good case against me. I mean, what about those explosives they found near where I was running? It'll be easy for them to say I stashed them there."

"Someone else could have planted them there," Frank pointed out. "Someone who was trying to set you up. And that someone had to know you were seeing Goodrich last night."

"I have to admit I was convinced you were guilty," Joe said to Andy. "But now I'm not so sure. You seem to really care about the company."

"I do care about it," Andy said. "Even though I don't work there anymore."

"The public defender said she thought Andy's case would be coming up for trial soon, maybe next week," Mrs. Quayle said, with an anxious look at Frank and Joe. "Will you really be able to prove Andy's innocence by then?"

"I hope so. But in any case, we can still get Andy

a good lawyer, and we'll keep on digging," Frank said to her.

"Sergeant Prescott thinks I'm guilty," Andy said, "and Goodrich has a lot of power in Pine Beach. He's likely to win."

"But what he hasn't counted on is us," said Joe, with a grin. Everyone laughed. Even Andy managed a small smile.

Frank said, "I think that what we need to do is launch a three-pronged investigation. And we're going to need some help. Iola, what's your brother doing now?"

"Chet's probably getting ready for tonight's Trusty rally. He's been named Newcomer of the Month, and he has to give a little speech to other newcomers, sort of a pep talk."

"Good," Frank said. "Then he can get started with his part of the investigation right away. He'll be the perfect person to find out things about the company from the inside. Callie, Iola—I'd like you to go to the rally, too, and pretend to be interested in becoming Trusty Teens."

"Us?" said Callie.

"Just go a few times. You don't actually have to join. See what you can dig up on Alison, and anybody else that might be important in this case."

"Oh, okay," Callie said. "Just as long as we don't have to join."

"I guess I'm in, too," Iola said. "I mean, when have I ever refused a little excitement?"

"Never," said Joe, smiling at her.

"Right," Frank said. "One of the first things Joe and I will do is poke around the Trusty warehouse to find out a few things about Goodrich and those cartons."

"I don't know who has the tougher job," Joe said, "us having to worry about tangling with Goodrich and those warehouse workers or Chet, Iola, and Callie having to face the Trusty Teens."

They all laughed and said goodbye to Andy and Mrs. Quayle, both of whom looked slightly less worried. Then Frank and Joe drove back to Bayport and parked in front of the Mortons' house. Iola and Callie pulled into the driveway a few seconds later.

"Where's the Teen of the Month?" Joe called up the stairs after they had entered the house.

"Oh, you heard," Chet said, coming to the landing. "And it's *Newcomer* of the Month. I've just been practicing my speech." Chet looked like anything but a Trusty Newcomer of the Month, standing there in a pair of worn khaki shorts and a short-sleeved sweatshirt.

"Come on down," Joe said. "We have something exciting to tell you."

"Is it more exciting than being named Newcomer of the Month?" Chet wanted to know as he pounded down the stairs.

"That depends on your point of view," said Frank with a little smile.

"Remember what I told you about Andy Quayle last night?" Iola said. "Well, we were just down in Pine Beach to see him. They arrested him, and we

43

got him out on bail. Now we're going to try to clear him."

Chet frowned. "It must be tough. Goodrich is pretty well liked around Pine Beach. He's helped hundreds of kids get off the streets and into selling Trusty products. With the money they've made from Trusty, they've been able to go to college, buy cars, set themselves up in business, lots of things."

"Haven't the Trusty Teens also made Goodrich wealthy?" asked Frank.

"I guess so," Chet said. "As executive manager of the East Coast branch, he gets a piece of everything."

"Maybe Goodrich has to lie to protect himself," suggested Joe. "He could stand to lose a lot if something fishy's going on and there's an investigation."

"That's true," Chet said, "but Goodrich seems like a good guy. I'm not convinced he's up to something crooked."

"What can you tell us about Vince Boggs?" said Frank.

"Well, I've gotten to know Boggs a little. He was the first guy I met at a Trusty rally. He's sort of taken me under his wing."

"And . . . ?" prompted Frank.

"And, I guess you want to know what's been going on between him and Goodrich? I'm not sure I ought to tell you. He asked me to keep it quiet."

"Come on, Chet, if it might help us with our investigation, tell us."

44

"Well, I don't know," Chet said. "Boggs has been seeing Goodrich's daughter, Denise, and Goodrich doesn't like it."

"Why not?" asked Joe.

"Beats me," Chet said. "Even Boggs says he doesn't know for sure. Anyway, their romance is going to be history real soon."

"How come?" Joe asked.

"Goodrich is sending her away to stay with relatives in California. She leaves tomorrow night."

"Is Boggs the kind of guy who'd get so mad at Goodrich that he'd blow up his warehouse?" Frank asked.

"I don't know him well enough to say," Chet replied.

"Well, why don't you try to get to know him better?" Frank said.

Then Iola told Chet what had happened with Alison Rosedale in front of the police station. "Do you know why Goodrich is avoiding her? He doesn't have a son who's dating her, does he?"

"No," said Chet, totally missing his sister's humor. "And I don't know why anybody wouldn't talk to Alison. She's gorgeous! You saw her."

"We don't exactly have an objective party here," Joe kidded.

"What do you know about Andy Quayle?" said Frank.

"I never actually met him," Chet said. "I've seen him a couple of times. I heard he's a real hard worker. He's not a show-off type like Alison or

Boggs. I was surprised when Iola told me he'd been fired."

"Why don't we all go to the Trusty complex together?" Joe suggested. "We'll drive. After we drop you off at the rally, we'll look around at the warehouse."

"Sounds okay to me," Chet said. "But don't go yet. I want you guys to see something first."

Chet disappeared upstairs into his room. Several minutes later, he returned and handed Frank a cardboard kit full of promotional sales literature and inspirational cassette tapes. "Take a look at these," Chet said. "You'll get a better idea of how the organization runs. I've got to go back upstairs and work on my speech. I'll see you guys later."

The Hardys, Callie, and Iola went into the dining room, where they spread the contents of the kit out onto the table. Most of the material listed ways to sell particular products: how to approach the customer, how to make the presentation, how to close the sale. But there were a couple of brochures that stressed over and over again what a great big happy family Trusty was, that it stressed cooperation above competition, that there was enough business and enough money for everybody if they just learned to develop their own positive mental attitude and customer base.

After the four of them finished reading all the materials, Frank and Joe got up to leave. Callie had been invited to have dinner at the Mortons. "We'll grab a bite to eat and stop back," said Joe.

"Be here by six-fifteen," called Chet, who had come back downstairs and was on his way to the kitchen for a predinner snack. "I don't want to be late."

As Frank and Joe drove home, they discussed the case.

"Okay, who have we got so far in the way of suspects?" Joe asked.

"Well, there's Boggs," replied Frank. "He's got a grudge against Goodrich. Alison Rosedale seems to want Andy Quayle out of Trusty as soon as possible. So she might have set him up." Frank pulled the van into the driveway of their house. He added, "Then there's Goodrich himself."

"But why would Goodrich want to blow up his own warehouse?"

Frank shook his head. "I don't know."

"Hey, look," Joe said as they headed toward the house. "Aunt Gertrude forgot to bring in the mail this morning." He jogged up to the mailbox and pulled out a long white envelope that was sticking partway out of the box. "Just one letter," he reported. "And it's addressed to us."

Joe ripped open the envelope. He removed a white sheet of paper, unfolded it, and read what was written on it. Then, silently, he held up the paper for Frank to read. The single sentence, made up of clumsily pasted-up letters, said:

DROP THE QUAYLE CASE . . . OR ELSE!

5 Trading Punches

When Frank and Joe went back to Chet and Iola's house after dinner, they showed their friends the note right away.

"You're not going to let a little thing like a threat scare you off, are you?" asked Chet.

"Come on, Chet, you know us better than that," Joe said.

"I think whoever's behind this is trying to do exactly what Chet says—just scare us off," said Frank.

"For now," Callie said. "The question is, when will this person start putting into action the 'or else' part of the threat?"

"Maybe we ought to go to the rally in my car," Chet suggested. "I mean, whoever sent that note might be tailing you."

"Whatever happened to 'You're not going to let a

little thing like a threat scare you off'?" Iola asked her brother. "Now let's get going, or else the Newcomer of the Month will be late."

They decided to take the Hardys' car after all. When they got to the Trusty complex, Frank and Joe dropped Chet and the girls off in the parking lot near the auditorium. "We'll probably be through before you are," Frank said to them, "so we'll wait around here for you. Look for the wagon."

"Right," Callie said. "See you later." Iola waved. Chet was already halfway to the auditorium.

Frank pulled the wagon alongside the warehouse, near where the explosion had taken place the night before. As they were about to get out of the car, Joe grabbed Frank's arm. "Look at that!" he whispered. Several workers were busy repairing the damaged portion of the building.

"They sure haven't wasted any time," Joe said. "I wonder if the fire marshal or an insurance adjuster has inspected the damage."

"Even if they have," Frank said, "it usually takes a few days for the paperwork to go through authorizing repairs."

"Goodrich must have gotten some fast action," Joe commented. "I guess what Andy and Chet said about him having pull in this town is true."

Just then one of the workers came over to them. He was young—in his early twenties—with a head of curly brown hair and a face covered with freckles.

49

"Can I help you guys?" he asked in a friendly voice.

"Oh, hi," Frank said casually. "We were here last night after the explosion. We just wanted to see what the damage looked like in the light."

"It's great that you guys were able to start working so quickly," said Joe.

"Yeah, well, Mr. Goodrich said he'd pay good overtime if we'd start today and work till dark," said the worker. "We got all the rubble out of here this afternoon. Now we're rebuilding the roof."

"Do you mind if we look around?" asked Frank.

"You guys can look all you want, but don't get too close. I don't want you to get hit with a piece of lumber. Hey, listen, I have to get back to work."

"Okay," said Frank. "Thanks a lot."

From where they stood, Frank and Joe could see a fire-scorched metal double door standing partly open. Beyond it was the blackened interior of a room maybe twenty feet square. It had been swept clean. The freckle-faced worker was finishing up the framing for a new roof above the door.

"From the way that thing went up last night, it looked like something pretty flammable had been stored there," Frank called up to him.

"Don't know," the worker said. "This room was always off-limits to me. Once I kidded the foreman about there being some kind of top-secret soap powder in here, and he got mad."

"Do you know if the fire investigator was here?" Joe asked.

50

"Not while we were," the worker answered. "But he might have come earlier."

Just then they became aware of heavy footsteps approaching. Turning around, they saw a tall, muscular redheaded man, who looked to be in his early twenties, barreling toward them.

He looked up. "Rogers!" he snapped in a deep voice. "Who are these kids?" He glared at Frank and Joe. "If they're looking for the rally, it's over in the auditorium."

"They're not here about the meeting," said the worker, Rogers. "They were up here last night right after the explosion."

"Now, look, guys," the redheaded man said, "I've only got one thing to say to you: Get lost! You don't belong here, and I don't want you bothering my workers."

"Cut it out, Carson," Rogers said. "They weren't bothering anybody. Give them a break."

"Are you trying to tell me my job?" Carson said with a note of menace in his voice. "Just get back to work." To Frank and Joe he yelled, "Move it!"

"We're going, we're going!" Joe yelled back, and he and Frank made tracks for their car.

"Now what?" Joe asked. "Our warehouse investigation turned out to be a real bust."

"Well, at least we got to sort of meet Del Carson, the foreman," said Frank.

Frank drove the wagon over to the parking lot by the auditorium where the rally was being held. Luckily, they found a parking spot close to the building. They sat in silence for a half hour while Joe checked his watch impatiently every few minutes.

"Let's go into the auditorium," he said, finally. "It's getting boring sitting here."

Frank was just about to answer when a crowd suddenly began to stream through the large double doors of the auditorium.

Everyone was talking excitedly and pointing back at the auditorium.

"That's no ordinary end-of-a-meeting crowd," Frank said. "Something's going on up there."

They jumped out of the car and ran toward the crowd. With more and more people—mostly teenagers—pouring out into the parking lot, they couldn't get too close to the building. Everyone seemed to want to get a better look at something that was happening inside the auditorium, near the door.

"What's going on?" Joe asked a girl with a dark ponytail.

"Didn't you see it? Mr. Goodrich attacked Vince Boggs, and now they're really going at it. I hope Goodrich knocks the stuffing out of Boggs. I don't know what this is all about, but Boggs is just too stuck-up. Who does he think he is, anyhow—even if he is so cute and smart and all. Go, Mr. Goodrich!" she shouted.

Frank and Joe elbowed their way through the crowd to try to get to the scene of the fight, but they were unsuccessful.

Then they heard voices yelling, "Let me go!" "Let me get him!" "Keep your hands off me!"

Another voice shouted, "Give Vince room to get up! Let him through!" It sounded like Chet!

Slowly the crowd moved aside to leave a narrow pathway in the middle. Through it, Frank could see Chet using a full-nelson restraining hold on wriggling Bob Goodrich while Vince Boggs struggled to his feet.

"Next time you won't be so lucky!" Goodrich screamed. "If I ever catch you around here again, I'm going to make mincemeat out of you and feed you to your computer!"

He jerked his head back toward Chet. "And your friend here is through, too. Let me go, you big ox!"

But Chet kept his hold on the red-faced manager.

"Goodbye Newcomer of the Month," murmured Joe.

Chet watched as Vince Boggs worked his way to the outer row of the crowd. Then, Chet slowly let go of Goodrich, who smoothed out the jacket of his suit and quickly went back inside the auditorium.

Chet jogged through the crowd, which was thinning out a little as a number of the kids followed Goodrich back into the building. "Vince!" he called. "Wait up!"

As he passed Frank and Joe, he nodded and held up a finger indicating they should wait. Boggs stopped and let Chet catch up with him. "Hey, guys," Chet called to Frank and Joe, "come over here! I want you to meet somebody.

"This is Vince Boggs, who I was telling you about before," Chet continued. "Vince, these are my best friends, Frank and Joe Hardy."

Vince Boggs was a slim, dark-haired young man with a friendly smile. He shook hands with the Hardys. Frank looked to see if Boggs had been hurt. His hair was slightly messed up, but otherwise he seemed okay.

"Thanks, Chet," Boggs said. "Without your help, I never would have gotten away from that maniac. I mean, I'm not much of a fighter, and he was acting like a real animal. And he doesn't have to worry about me bothering him again, either," Boggs added. "It's just not worth it. I'll find some other way to make money to buy my lab equipment. And I'll find somebody else's daughter to go out with."

"Wait a minute," Frank said. "Where are Callie and Iola? Did they come out with you?"

"I don't know where they are," Chet said. "They must still be inside, I guess."

They watched as the last few kids went back into the building, then they waited with their eyes fixed on the doors. In a few minutes, Callie and Iola came walking outside.

"Hi, guys," Iola said. "We saw the whole thing, but we still don't believe it. First Chet does the whole Morton family proud as Trusty Newcomer of the Month, then he gets into a wrestling match with the guy handing out the award! You really put Goodrich out of commission, Chet."

"I knew there was a good reason why I spent so much time developing your potential at Trusty," Boggs said. "Although it didn't pay off the way I'd thought. I hope you'll still come by my place later this week, even though I won't be helping you with your sales strategy."

"Sure," said Chet.

"Listen," Boggs said to Frank and Joe, "I hear you might be interested in some of the stuff I've got in my lab. Why don't you come, too?" He said goodbye quickly without waiting for an answer and headed off through the parking lot.

"What is he talking about?" Joe asked. "What stuff?"

"I told Boggs you were real hotshot scientists."

"Why did you do a thing like that?" asked Frank.

"Because I thought it would be easier to get you an invitation to his house. Easier than joining Trusty, anyhow."

"We might have to join," Joe said, "since you blew it."

"You can't," Iola said. "Goodrich would never hire you now. But guess what? Callie and I were invited to Alison Rosedale's cosmetics demonstration on Tuesday."

"Good work!" Frank said. "How did you manage it so quickly?"

"It wasn't exactly hard," Callie said. "Alison introduced herself. I guess she was so busy threatening Andy Quayle this morning in front of the police station that she didn't even see us. Tonight, when we entered the auditorium, she assumed that we wanted to join the sales force and she gave us the invitation. Remember, if we join, she gets a percentage."

They all headed back to the station wagon. "By the way, Chet," Frank said, "did you get to give your speech?"

"Yes," Chet said with a sigh. "I gave it."

"Barely," Iola added. "And I have to admit it was a pretty good one, even if he did go on a little too long about the virtues of Trusty Brite Laundry Detergent."

"Cut it out, Iola. You know I didn't," Chet said. "Anyway, the whole talk only lasted about two minutes."

"That's because he left half of his cue cards at home," Iola said teasingly.

"If I didn't know my sister better," Chet said, "I'd swear she stole them. Anyway, I knew the whole thing by heart."

"I didn't remember the ending going that way from when you rehearsed it," Iola said with a smirk.

"Yeah, and speaking of the end of my speech, that's how the whole thing with Boggs and Goodrich got started," said Chet.

"What do you mean?" Frank asked.

"Are you saying that *you* caused the fight?" asked Joe.

"It wasn't my fault," Chet protested. "Really. I only gave Boggs credit for getting me going on the right foot. Some of the kids in the audience began shouting, 'Boggs! Boggs!' so he came up onto the stage."

Chet shook his head. "It all happened so fast. Goodrich ordered Boggs off, and when he wouldn't go, Goodrich sort of went berserk. Boggs tried to shake him off, but Goodrich wouldn't leave him alone. They made it all the way to the door, where Boggs managed to take a couple of swings at Goodrich. Goodrich slugged him back. I think he would have beaten up Boggs badly if I or somebody else hadn't stopped him."

"If that's the way Goodrich treats people," Iola said, "it's no wonder he has to worry about somebody wanting to blow him up."

"Goodrich couldn't be *that* mad at Boggs just for dating his daughter," Frank said. "I'd really like to know what's setting him off."

"He might just be off, period," said Joe.

Chet and the girls got into the station wagon. But before Frank and Joe could follow, a late-model silver-colored sedan pulled up beside them and came to an abrupt halt. As the window rolled down they made out Goodrich's face.

"You two sure turn up at all the right moments," he said. He glanced over at Chet in the station wagon. "And I see you've got my favorite hulk with you, too."

"We were just picking up some friends from the rally," Joe said.

"Oh, yeah?" Goodrich said. "Well, that was your beefy friend's last rally."

Frank and Joe ignored Goodrich's comments about Chet. Instead Frank asked, "Now that we've run into you like this, do you mind if we ask you a couple of questions? Something's bothering us about last night."

"Yes, I mind," snapped Goodrich. "And I don't like the way you guys keep showing up around here, sticking your noses into my business." He leaned out the window. "I want you to know I've instructed my security guards to be on the lookout for you. If they see you here again, they're to call the police, who will arrest you for trespassing. Got that?" With those words, Goodrich rolled up the window and drove away with a lurch.

6 Getting the Goods

"So, what do we do *now*?" Joe asked. "Snooping around at the warehouse is out. And the whole Trusty complex is off-limits to us now."

Frank thought for a minute. Then he said, "I think we should pay a little visit to Goodrich's office."

"Didn't you hear what Goodrich just said? If he sees us here again, he'll have us arrested for trespassing!"

"I didn't say Goodrich would be in his office when we visited it," Frank said carefully. "And we'll have to come up with a way to get past the security guards."

"What do you think we'll find in Goodrich's office, anyway?" asked Joe.

Frank shrugged. "I'm not sure, but remember what Andy Quayle said? He said he saw Del Carson, the foreman, looking through Goodrich's desk. I have a feeling Carson wasn't really looking for his paycheck."

"Hey, are you guys going to stand around there all night?" Chet called out. "If you are, toss us the keys to the car, okay?"

Frank and Joe walked to the station wagon and got in. As Frank drove toward Bayport, he and his brother filled in their friends on their conversation with Goodrich, leaving out his comments about Chet, and on their plan to search Goodrich's office.

"I think our best bet would be to get there early in the morning," Joe said. "Before Goodrich arrives."

"Chet, do you know what time he gets to work?" Frank asked.

"Goodrich comes in at around eight-thirty," Chet replied. "Everyone else, including his secretary, usually shows up at nine."

The Hardys decided to get there at seven-thirty. They figured that would give them plenty of time to look through Goodrich's desk, search the rest of his office, and get out before he arrived.

"But how are you going to get past the security guards?" Callie asked. "Goodrich probably gave them your description."

"Hey, no problem," Chet said with a grin. "I've got all kinds of Trusty T-shirts, hats, and jackets in different sizes. I have blank IDs, too, all with Goodrich's signature on them. You know, for all those new salespeople I was supposed to recruit."

"It might work," Frank said, nodding. "But we'd still be taking a chance."

"Sounds like a good plan to me," Iola said. "Anyway," she added, "there are a lot of brown-haired, brown-eyed guys in the world who look like you, Frank." She turned to Joe. "And a lot of blond, blue-eyed guys like *you*."

"And I always thought I was one of a kind," Joe protested laughingly.

They dropped Callie off first, since she had to spend some time with an aunt and uncle who were visiting the Shaws. When the Hardys, Iola, and Chet got to the Mortons' house, Chet gave Frank and Joe two Trusty shirts and two IDs. He also gave them two cartons containing samples of Trusty cleaning products and cosmetics.

"Tell the guards that Goodrich asked you to bring these product kits over for an early-morning meeting," Chet told them. "Goodrich has meetings like that all the time."

"Let's just hope he doesn't plan to have one tomorrow morning," said Frank.

At seven-thirty the next morning, wearing Trusty T-shirts and ID tags that said they were "Chris Knight" and "Randy Potter," the Hardys parked their van in the lot of a diner across the road from the Trusty complex. Then they headed for the part of the complex that housed Goodrich's office. They were stopped at the door by two security guards.

Frank and Joe told the guards their made-up

story. After checking out the ID tags and looking carefully through the sample-product kits, one of the guards ushered Frank and Joe into the building.

"Where do you need to drop off this stuff?" asked the guard. "Conference room?"

"Mr. Goodrich said we should set up a display in his office," Frank said.

Joe added, "He's meeting with some executives from the Trusty corporate offices in Illinois, and he decided his office would be more comfortable."

The guard seemed satisfied with that explanation. He unlocked the door to Goodrich's office and let them inside.

Frank and Joe gave the guard time to get back outside the building. Then Joe closed the office door quietly. "Whew!" he said. "I can't believe we got away with that story!"

"Keep your voice down," Frank cautioned, "and let's get to work. Those guards are going to get pretty suspicious if we're in here too long."

While Frank looked through Goodrich's desk, Joe checked out the drawers of a file cabinet that was standing by the window. He was looking through the bottom drawer when Frank gave a low whistle. Joe glanced up. Frank was staring at a piece of paper he had taken out of the top drawer of Goodrich's desk. "What is it?" Joe asked.

But before Frank could answer him, a voice on the other side of the door said loudly, "What do you guys think I'm paying you for, anyway? You're supposed to be watching my warehouse, not drinking coffee in the hall!"

It was Goodrich!

Frank quickly jammed the paper back into the desk drawer. Then he and Joe looked around desperately for a place to hide.

Suddenly, Joe spotted a door to the left of the desk. Frank saw it, too. Without stopping to consider where it might lead, or whether or not it was locked, the brothers picked up the product kits and headed for the door. Joe turned the handle.

Luckily, the door wasn't locked. Frank and Joe dashed into the other room and closed the door behind them gently just as Goodrich entered his office.

The room the Hardys were in was dark and stuffy. After their eyes had gotten somewhat used to the darkness, they could see they were in a small, windowless conference room. Joe tried the door on the other side of the room, but it was locked. He walked back to Frank and shrugged.

Through the door leading to Goodrich's office, they heard the Trusty manager begin to speak. It sounded as though he was dictating letters.

A few minutes later, they heard the outside door to Goodrich's office open, then close. A girl's voice said, "Dad, we have to talk. I heard what you did to Vince last night, and I want an explanation."

"I don't owe you any explanations, Denise," Goodrich said angrily. "That two-bit fortune hunter is out of your life for good. You should be glad. I've done you a favor."

"Don't you think that Vince, or anybody, could like me just for myself, not because I'm your daughter? Your head is so big, I'm surprised the rest of you can fit into this office at the same time!"

"Now, you listen to me, young lady," Goodrich snapped. "You're going to California tonight. I want you as far away from Boggs as possible."

Denise didn't answer. Instead, the Hardys heard her slam the door behind her as she left. There was a minute of silence, then Goodrich went back to his dictation.

Fifteen minutes later, there was a knock at the door. "Come in!" called Goodrich.

"What is it, Alison?" Goodrich said in an exasperated tone of voice. "I'm busy."

Frank and Joe looked at each other. Joe mouthed the words "Alison Rosedale."

"You know very well what it is," Alison said. "Have you thought about my little proposition?"

"Sure, for about two seconds," Goodrich replied.

"Well, you'd better think about it some more," Alison said, "or else you know what I'll do. And time's running out. Either way you'll pay. You decide which way it'll be, and let me know."

"Listen, you're not calling the shots here," Goodrich said. "Boggs thought he was, and look where it got him. I could just as easily throw you out, too."

"Don't bluff me, Bob. We both know I hold the

high card. Today's Monday. I'm going to give you until the end of the week to make up your mind."

Frank and Joe heard Alison slam the door even harder than Denise had.

Goodrich returned to his dictation for a while. Then for the next fifteen minutes or so, the only sounds Frank and Joe heard were papers shuffling and drawers opening and closing.

Then they heard the door to Goodrich's office open again.

"Everything ready, Carson?" Goodrich said.

"All set."

"Good. Maury is expecting the truck in an hour, so don't disappoint him."

"I still would rather do it after dark," said Carson.

"I know," Goodrich answered. "But this time it just doesn't work out that way."

"Suppose somebody sees us?"

"What will they see, some cartons of soap powder being unloaded? Stop worrying."

"That's easy for you to say. You get to sit behind your desk while I'm out there taking the risks."

"Look," Goodrich said, "if it'll make you feel any better, I'll come over to the warehouse with you and see that you get away all right."

The Hardys heard Goodrich get up and the door close again. The office was silent.

"Let's get out of here," said Frank.

"What if those security guards are still around?" asked Joe.

"That's a risk we'll have to take. Anyway, if they see us, we'll make up some story. And we'd better leave the sample kits in here."

They walked out of the conference room into Goodrich's office, then opened the office door quietly and peered out. There was nobody around. The security guards were no longer stationed at the front door.

Breathing huge sighs of relief, Frank and Joe hurriedly left the building and headed toward the road and their van.

As they neared the road, they saw a Trusty Home Products truck at the foot of the driveway to their left. Frank and Joe recognized the red-haired driver as Del Carson, the Trusty foreman. The truck hesitated a moment, then turned right onto the road.

"I think we should follow that truck," Frank said. "What do you say, Joe?"

"I say, let's do it!"

They ran across the road to the diner, jumped into the van, and quickly pulled onto the road. There wasn't much traffic, so Frank followed the Trusty truck from a reasonable distance, allowing a couple of cars to get between the truck and the van.

"By the way," Joe said as they drove along. "What was that paper you found in Goodrich's desk?"

"It was a carbon copy of an invoice for a carton of Trusty Brite Laundry Detergent," Frank replied.

"That seems innocent enough," said Joe.

"Maybe. But there wasn't any date, price, or name listed on the carbon. Just the number five."

"That's strange," Joe said. "Was there a signature on it?"

Frank nodded. "Andy Quayle's."

Now it was Joe's turn to let out a whistle.

The road bypassed the main business section of Pine Beach, circling around and hugging the shoreline. After being trapped in the hot, airless conference room, the Hardys were grateful for the cool breeze coming off the water. Frank kept the truck in sight at all times.

At a fork in the road, the Trusty truck turned left onto a blacktop road that continued near the water to the end of a sparsely inhabited peninsula called Near Isle. Scrub pines grew more densely along this stretch. There were few houses near the road—just mailboxes at the outlets of sandy driveways that went back several hundred feet to secluded summer cottages.

Frank followed the truck for a mile or so and then watched it make a left turn down one of the sandy lanes between two stands of pines. Frank pulled over onto the shoulder of the road and waited a few minutes before going in after the truck.

"Where are they going?" Joe asked. "We're close to the water. Are they planning to dump something?"

"He's heading toward the water, all right," Frank

replied. "This lane is probably a dead end. If it is, they'll hear the van coming. Let's leave it here and walk down."

The air was fragrant with the smell of pine trees, but it was also thick with tension. After following the lane for about a quarter of a mile, the Hardys suddenly spotted a small clearing. In the clearing stood the Trusty truck.

Frank and Joe headed into the woods by the side of the lane, where they wouldn't be seen but would still have a good view of the truck. After a few minutes of watching and waiting for signs of life from the truck, Frank whispered to Joe, "Let's try to get into that truck."

The Hardys made their way quickly and noiselessly to the truck. There was a padlock on the sliding door, but it wasn't locked. As quietly as possible Joe removed the padlock, grabbed the handle, and slid the door open until there was just room enough to squeeze inside the back of the truck. When they were inside, Joe reached out, replaced the padlock, and shut the door so that it was only open a crack.

"No sense leaving ourselves wide open in case somebody comes along while we're in here," he whispered.

The truck was loaded neatly with cartons, but Frank and Joe had enough space to move around between them. They turned on their pocket flashlights and began to examine the cartons. The labels all read, "Trusty Brite Laundry Detergent."

"I have a feeling these cartons aren't full of laundry detergent," Frank said.

"I have a feeling you're right," replied Joe. "But there's only one way to find out what really *is* in these cartons." He took a Swiss army knife out of one of his pockets and slit open a carton at the seams. He reached inside and pulled out a small square-shaped package wrapped in plastic.

"What *is* that stuff?" Frank asked. "It looks like modeling clay."

Joe shook his head slowly, "It's not clay," he said. "And it's not laundry detergent, either. Even though, with this stuff, you *could* get an extra bang out of your laundry."

"What are you talking about?" Frank asked.

"I'm positive that this stuff is Splode-All. I heard one of Dad's FBI friends talking about it at dinner a few months ago. You were out with Callie."

"So, what is it?" asked Frank.

"It's an illegal substance that's used with other materials to make high-quality explosive devices," Joe replied. "I bet we're sitting on a whole shipment of it!"

"So that's what Goodrich is up to," Frank said. "He's probably been storing this stuff somewhere in the Trusty warehouse. I wonder who they're buying it from—and who they're selling it to."

"And who's in on it," Joe added, "besides Goodrich and Carson."

"Wait a minute," Frank said. "I just thought of something. Remember what Andy said about the workers at the warehouse handling cartons as if they were full of glass?"

"So?"

"So, *those* cartons couldn't have been full of Splode-All," replied Frank. "That stuff isn't dangerous on its own, right?"

Joe stared at his brother. "You think Goodrich is dealing in explosive devices, too?"

"I think it's a very real possibility," replied Frank.

The brothers looked around the truck uneasily, wondering which, if any, of the cartons contained explosives.

"I think we ought to get out of here," Joe said. "I don't like the idea of sitting in the back of a truck that could decide to blow its top."

"That makes two of us," Frank answered. "But let's take an unopened carton of the Splode-All with us. If we show this one as evidence to Sergeant Prescott, he can always say we put the Splode-All in there ourselves."

"Just one thing," Joe said. "What if I'm wrong about this stuff? What if we haul it back and it turns out to be some weird new kind of soap powder?"

"Then we're all washed up," Frank said with a grim smile. "But it's a chance we have to take."

"I just thought of something else," Joe said. "How do we know which of these cartons contains Splode-All and which ones might be packed with explosives?"

They looked at the cartons, finally deciding to take the one directly under the one they'd opened.

Just as they lifted the carton and were about to leave the truck, they heard voices.

Joe pointed to a tall stack of cartons toward the front of the truck. Frank nodded, and the brothers crept over and crouched down behind the cartons, waiting as the voices came nearer.

"Goodrich is getting worried," said a voice that Frank and Joe recognized as Del Carson's. "First there was that Quayle kid. Who knows if the cops can make Goodrich's claim stick? Now there are those two kid detectives nosing around. So far he doesn't think they've found anything—or that they ever will."

"Kid detectives?" said another voice. "How does he know? Did they flash their cards in his face?"

"No," Carson said. "He had them checked out."

"With who? Their Boy Scout troop?" replied the second man with a snorting laugh.

Frank didn't recognize the second man's voice, but he tried to let it register so he could remember it later if he had to. It was raspy and nasal, and some of the sentences ended with a little high-pitched wheeze.

The voices stopped for a while, and the Hardys could hear the faint sound of a boat engine. The engine noise grew louder.

"Right on time, Carson, if you consider five minutes late on time," said the second man.

"It's close enough for me, Maury," said Carson.

"Well," Maury said, "let's start unloading those boxes."

The Hardy Brothers froze as the rear door of the truck opened with a metallic roar.

They were trapped!

7 Police Action

Frank and Joe waited silently behind the cartons. They knew what they would do the moment Carson and Maury came close enough. The brothers tensed their bodies, getting ready to spring out of their crouch and jump past the two men.

They listened for the sounds of unloading. Instead, they heard Maury say, "You know, Carson, I think we ought to get Benson to pitch in and help. Let's go and get him off the boat."

Footsteps retreated across the clearing, and the voices trailed off to whispers.

Frank and Joe held their breaths until they heard the rustle of bodies moving through the woods at the edge of the clearing. Then the sounds died out altogether. Joe, still clutching the carton, and Frank climbed out of the truck and sprinted back down the lane to their van.

Joe placed the carton carefully on the floor of the passenger side of the van. "I'm pretty sure this is the Splode-All stuff, but we can't take any chances."

"You've got to admit, though, that bringing Prescott a carton of explosives would really make him listen to our story," said Frank.

"The Splode-All will be enough. He'll have to listen to us," Joe replied.

Frank nodded. "But Prescott is going to have to move fast. As soon as Goodrich and Carson find out that their cargo has been tampered with, they'll start covering their tracks. We've got to hope Prescott can find some incriminating evidence at the Trusty warehouse. Near Isle is way out of his jurisdiction. I'm not even sure if it has a local police force. The county probably patrols this area. And since the stuff is being transported by boat, the Coast Guard may have to be dragged into the picture, too."

Frank and Joe retraced their route back to Pine Beach and parked across the street from the police station. When they entered the station, they asked for Sergeant Prescott. The police officer at the front desk nodded in the direction of the squad room.

In the squad room they found Prescott, head down over some paperwork, at his desk in the corner. He looked up at them and frowned. "I was sure I'd seen the last of you two, but I guess I was wrong." He looked at the carton in Joe's arms. "So,

74

what are you doing here? Trying to sell some Trusty laundry detergent to the police force?"

Frank and Joe ignored Prescott's nasty remarks. Instead Frank said, "Listen, Sergeant, we have some important information for you. We think we're on to something you should know about."

He told Prescott about following Carson in the Trusty truck out to Near Isle and what they had found. Then Joe handed Prescott the carton. "Be careful," he warned. "We're almost one-hundred-percent sure this is Splode-All, but it might be explosive, too."

Sergeant Prescott gave Joe a skeptical look. Then he slit open the carton with a razor blade and looked at the contents. Frank and Joe looked into the carton, too, and saw that it contained what Joe had identified as the Splode-All.

"You're saying that this stuff here is—what did you call it?—'Splode-All,'" said Prescott.

"That's right," Joe replied.

Prescott shook his head. "Well, I've never heard of it. How do I know this stuff isn't some new kind of laundry detergent? If you were real detectives, you'd know better than to come in here with a carton of soap and a cooked-up story about some kind of smuggling operation."

Frank and Joe opened their mouths to protest, but Prescott didn't give them the opportunity.

"I've known Bob Goodrich for thirty years, since we were boys together in this town. I can vouch for

75

the man. He'd never get involved in something like this."

The Hardys couldn't tell Prescott that they'd been hiding next door to Goodrich's office when they discovered that Goodrich was not only involved but in charge. Instead, Frank just said, "Please, Sergeant, we're strongly suggesting that you check out our story."

"And that you have the stuff in this carton analyzed," Joe added.

Prescott fixed the Hardys with a penetrating stare.

"Listen, kids like you with nothing to do all summer besides play amateur detective don't tell me how I should lead my investigations," he said evenly. "I'm satisfied that Goodrich is telling the truth and that Quayle is guilty. Do you have a better suspect?"

"No," Joe said. "But maybe the Trusty explosion was just an accident. If explosives were being kept in the warehouse, maybe it was just a coincidence that they went off when Quayle was at the complex."

Prescott narrowed his eyes. "And what were those explosives we found by the side of the road? Just coincidence, too? Look, when you get some real evidence, come back and see me. Until then, I no more believe that Goodrich is involved in selling explosives than that my aunt Prudence is. Nice seeing you again, boys. Now, why don't you leave so I can finish this paperwork and go home. I'm already on two hours' overtime." He pushed the carton toward them, picked up a form, and began to fill it in.

It was a dismissal, flat and final.

"Isn't there something we can do to get Prescott to take us seriously?" Joe asked in a frustrated tone as the brothers left the police station and headed toward their van.

"Maybe I ought to have Chief Collig from Bayport call him," Frank said thoughtfully. Then he shook his head. "Forget it. I just remembered that the chief's on vacation. He and his wife are on a cruise somewhere."

"Just like our other character reference—Dad," said Joe. "Well, what do we do now?"

"I don't know," Frank said. "Right now, I can't think of anybody else to show this stuff to. Maybe we just ought to take the evening off and think about this case some more."

As Frank and Joe sat talking in their van, Prescott came out of the station and approached a tan late-model European sports car.

"Nice car," Joe commented as he and his brother watched Prescott unlock the door.

"Yeah," Frank replied. "Expensive, too. I wonder how a sergeant on a small-town police force can afford a car like that. He's got to have another source of money."

He and Joe looked at each other. "An illegal source?" asked Joe.

Frank suddenly started up the van. "Look, Prescott is leaving. Let's follow him."

Prescott proved to be easy to tail. He drove slowly down Main Street. About a mile out of downtown Pine Beach, his right-turn directional signal flashed and the sports car turned into a driveway leading to a neat, white clapboard cottage with green shutters. The Hardys pulled over to the curb, a few houses away.

Frank and Joe waited a few minutes, then got out of their van. The sun was setting and the sky shone violet and orange at the horizon. On the heavily tree-lined street, however, night seemed to have already come.

The Hardys crept up the drive along a line of bushes that divided the white clapboard cottage from the house next door. Then they skittered to the side window of the front room, where they'd seen a light. The window sash had been raised, enough so that Frank and Joe could peer in through the screen. They saw Prescott standing in the middle of the room with a stack of mail in his hand. He strode over to a leatherette recliner and lowered himself into it.

Prescott flipped the letters onto a table next to the chair and opened up a catalog of expensive-looking merchandise. His eyes lingered over the picture of some item that the Hardys couldn't make out. He grinned and folded back the page.

Still carrying the catalog, Prescott got up and

walked toward the back of the house. Outside, Frank and Joe followed. They saw a light come streaming out through a window in the back and headed for it. Crouching below the lighted window, they were able to look into Prescott's kitchen. Prescott was getting something out of the refrigerator. All of a sudden he shut the door and walked over to the window.

Frank and Joe dropped to the ground, hoping Prescott hadn't spotted them. They heard the window lock snap open and the sound of the window being raised as far as it would go.

"Gotta get that central air-conditioning unit installed!" Prescott muttered.

Frank and Joe waited a minute before resuming their former positions, crouched below the window on either side.

Suddenly the phone rang. "Yeah?" Prescott said. "Is it set for tonight? . . . Eleven? Good . . . Will Goodrich be there? . . . No? . . . Well, that figures. Anyway, as long as you and I get what's owed to us, what do we care, right? . . . Yeah, you'll get your share, don't worry. Okay, keep me informed . . . Right."

Prescott hung up the phone, and the Hardys stared at each other in amazement. Was Prescott involved in Goodrich's smuggling operation? And if so, how?

Joe motioned to Frank that he wanted to leave. There was a lot for the two of them to talk over, and they couldn't do it hiding under Prescott's window. But Frank shook his head and indicated that they should stay put.

Frank's wait-and-see tactic paid off. Just as Prescott was putting a frozen TV dinner into the toaster-oven, the phone rang again.

"Oh, it's you, Bob," Prescott said. "Well, now, listen. Those Hardy kids came to me today with some real interesting stuff about your little operation. I can either follow it up on my own, or you and I can have a nice chat about how to handle it."

Prescott spent a minute or so just listening, then he said, "Look, I know you don't want any trouble, but those kids have got to be stopped. They've been warned once. I guess they didn't want to take the hint. Now it's time to get them off our case *permanently!*"

8 Special Delivery

Prescott banged down the receiver and walked out of the kitchen. Frank and Joe beat a hasty retreat back to the street.

When the Hardys were safe inside the van and on their way home, Joe said, "So that's why he doesn't want to listen to us. He's working with Goodrich." Joe looked at his brother. "Maybe we should go to Prescott's superiors with our story."

"What superiors?" replied Frank. "There's only Chief Rudin, and you heard Prescott say the night of the explosion that the chief was going on vacation the next day."

"That's a pretty convenient setup for Goodrich —having a partner on the police force," said Joe.

"Or maybe Prescott muscled his way in. Somebody may have tipped him off."

"But who?" asked Joe.

"That's what we've got to find out."

When Frank and Joe got home, Chet was waiting for them. He had come right after dinner, and Aunt Gertrude had coaxed him into staying with an offer of peach pie. She had then gone off to her weekly bridge game.

"Where have you guys been?" Chet asked. "I wanted to tell you in person that we've all been invited over to Vince Boggs's house tomorrow."

When Frank and Joe didn't respond with any enthusiasm, Chet said, "Okay, okay, maybe it's not the most exciting news in town, but you did tell me to move in on him."

"Sorry, Chet," Frank said. "It's just that it's been a long day. We discovered a lot of things that have gotten us thinking and worrying."

Frank told Chet about the various conversations he and Joe had overheard in Goodrich's office, about following the Trusty truck and what they found inside it, and about their discovery of Prescott's involvement.

When Frank had finished his rundown of the day's events, Chet said, "You know, I'll bet that whatever is happening at eleven tonight is going on at the Trusty warehouse. Why don't you just drop over there and have a look for yourselves?"

"Good idea," Frank said. "And let's take our infrared camera," he said to Joe. "If we play it right, we may be able to get some pictures to use as evidence."

"And, Chet," Frank continued, "we really are glad you got us that invitation to Boggs's house. I'd still like to know why he and Goodrich hate each other so much. It can't just be because of Goodrich's daughter."

"Hey, Chet," Joe said. "Want to come with us tonight?"

"Can't," Chet replied. "I've got a movie date." He looked at his watch. "In fact, if I don't get a move on, I'm going to be late for it."

"Who's your date?" Joe asked. "Anybody we know?"

"You sort of know her," replied Chet. "It's Alison Rosedale."

"What!" Frank and Joe said at the same time.

"How did you manage to get a date with Alison Rosedale?" Frank wanted to know.

"Well, it's not *really* a date," Chet admitted sheepishly. "I was returning my Trusty kits to the office today, and she was there. She mentioned that she and some Trusty friends were meeting at the movies tonight and she asked me if I wanted to come, too."

"See if you can get any information out of her," Frank said.

"I'll try," Chet said. "But it won't be easy with four other people around." He got up to leave. "I'll let you know what happened when I see you tomorrow morning."

After Chet had gone, Frank and Joe fixed them-

83

selves some sandwiches from the meatloaf Aunt Gertrude had made for dinner. They ate hurriedly, then they headed back outside to the van.

"I'm beginning to forget what Bayport looks like," Joe commented as they started driving toward Pine Beach and the Trusty complex.

"I know what you mean," said Frank.

The Hardys reached the Trusty complex a few minutes after ten. As they passed the main entrance, what they could see of the building and the parking lot looked dark. Frank and Joe wondered where Goodrich's security guards were.

About thirty yards past the complex Frank made a U-turn. He pulled into the diner parking lot across the road from the Trusty complex.

Frank and Joe walked up the driveway, heading to the warehouse side of the Trusty complex. Their progress was slow and careful, and they kept looking around to see if any security guards were in the area.

Finally, they reached the truck bays, where they hid behind some large storage bins and waited.

Ten-thirty came, then passed. Soon it was a quarter to eleven . . . then eleven-thirty. There were no signs of life.

"Maybe Chet guessed wrong," Joe said. "Maybe whatever Prescott was talking about is happening someplace else."

"Why don't we have a quick look around and then go?" suggested Frank.

"We might as well," Joe said. "This isn't getting us anywhere."

Just as Joe was about to dart out of their hiding place, Frank whispered, "Joe! Get back!"

Joe quickly ducked back behind the storage bin as the sound of an approaching truck grew louder. When the truck reached the warehouse, it pulled past where the Hardys were hiding, stopped, and backed up to the building. It was a large tractor-trailer. In the glow from its lights, the Hardys noticed that there appeared to be no writing on it whatever.

Frank and Joe moved around to where they would have a better view. Suddenly the truck's horn sounded, and they jumped at the noise. After a couple of minutes, the door from the building to the dock opened, and out strode Del Carson and another man. Frank wondered if the other man was Maury.

As they came out, two men emerged from the cab of the tractor-trailer. All four of them met next to the driver's door.

"You're late," Carson said angrily. "It's a good thing Maury and I had some paperwork to take care of in the office. Otherwise I would have been at the dock waiting for you. And I *hate* to be kept waiting."

The driver muttered an excuse about the traffic.

"Yeah? Well, that's your problem, not mine," Carson said sneeringly. "Now let's get this stuff unloaded."

The second trucker approached the rear of the trailer, hoisted himself up on the loading dock, and opened the back of the trailer. The inside was piled with cartons. All the cartons that Frank and Joe could see were unlabeled.

Carson said, "We'll bring the stuff in through here." He pointed to the door. "I'll get a cart from inside." He disappeared, followed by Maury. Carson returned a few minutes later, alone, with a motorized cart.

Frank and Joe watched as the trailer was unloaded and the cartons were piled carefully onto the cart. As each cartload was completed, Carson would take it inside, where he and Maury apparently unloaded it.

The whole process took about an hour. Frank carefully took pictures with his tiny infrared camera.

After the trailer was completely unloaded, the two truckers got back in the cab and the tractor-trailer pulled away from the bay.

Frank and Joe kept still in their hiding place. There was no sign of Carson or Maury. Suddenly, the door to the dock opened. Carson and Maury came out of the warehouse and walked down the driveway to the Trusty parking field.

After allowing Carson and Maury ten minutes to clear out, Frank and Joe decided it was safe for them to make their getaway. They hurried down the driveway. All of a sudden, they heard the motor of a truck start up behind them. They turned around, trying to see where the noise was coming from. At that moment, a pair of high-beam headlights flashed on, and a large truck started speeding down the driveway directly at them.

Frank and Joe raced into the parking field as the truck bore down on them.

"Scatter!" shouted Frank.

The truck swerved, first toward Frank, then toward Joe. The brothers barely had time to think or to get their bearings. Then Frank spotted a low brick wall that separated the parking field from the grassy slope heading down to the road. Joe was halfway across the lot.

"Joe!" Frank yelled. "The wall! Just get to the wall and dive!"

From their opposite sides of the parking field, Frank and Joe ran toward the same section of the wall. The truck bore down on them.

Suddenly Frank tripped and fell headlong onto the blacktop. Joe dove on top of his brother, pulling Frank with him out of the truck's path.

The truck screeched to a halt, circled, and headed for the Hardys again. They scrambled to their feet and ran toward the wall. The truck sped after them.

Frank and Joe both made desperate head-first dives over the wall. A second later, they heard a loud crash as the truck slammed into the wall.

"That was a close one," Joe said after he'd sat up and caught his breath.

"I know that guy just tried to kill us," he added, "but maybe we should see how badly he's hurt."

Frank shook his head. "Forget it. We don't have to," he said.

"What do you mean?" Joe asked with a surprised look.

"I mean that there wasn't anyone driving that truck!"

9 Scientific Method

"What!" exclaimed Joe. He sat up straight and stared at his brother. "How do you know?"

"Before I tripped and fell, I got a good look at the truck's cab. There wasn't anybody inside it."

The brothers got to their feet and headed for their van. As they were driving back to Bayport, Joe said, "I don't get it. How could a truck drive itself?"

"The only way I can think of is by some remote-control device," replied Frank.

"Which means that someone was at Trusty tonight aiming that truck at us," Joe said.

"Right," Frank said with a nod. "And that someone must know a lot about electronics. Programming a truck to respond like that would take a lot of know-how."

"Do you think we ought to report this?" asked Joe.

"Who to?" said Frank.

"Well, we know that Prescott isn't on duty," Joe said. "There must be somebody else at the station. That Sergeant Clement, maybe."

"I don't know if we can trust him not to go blabbing to Prescott," Frank replied.

"I guess you're right," said Joe, sighing.

"You know," Frank said, "I just thought of something. If Prescott gets off work in the early evening, what was he doing responding to the call Saturday night at Trusty? It was after eleven."

"Overtime?" said Joe.

"Maybe. But he just could have been in the neighborhood," said Frank.

"Doing what?"

"Good question, Frank said. "But let's not try to answer it tonight. I'm bushed. I need to get some sleep."

"Same here," Joe said. "Like you told Chet before, it's been a long day."

The next morning, as Frank and Joe were eating breakfast, the phone rang. Frank went to answer it.

"You guys want to pick me up in your van to drive out to Vince Boggs's house?" said Chet. "That way, Iola can take the car. She and Callie have that cosmetics demonstration at Alison Rosedale's today. And speaking of Alison," Chet continued, "I couldn't get any information out of her last night. Every time I brought up

90

Goodrich, Boggs, or Trusty, she'd change the subject."

"Did you pick up anything from anybody else about Trusty? Any gossip?"

"Nope," replied Chet. "Just the usual rave reviews about how great the company is. Too bad the movie we saw didn't rate reviews like that!"

"Well, thanks for trying," Frank said. "We'll see what Iola and Callie can come up with today." He added, "We'll pick you up at around ten."

After breakfast, Frank and Joe spent an hour developing the film they had shot of the delivery to the Trusty Warehouse the night before. Then they picked up Chet and drove to Havenhurst, where Vince Boggs lived. On the way, they told Chet what had happened the night before.

Havenhurst was a pretty, old-fashioned village, popular with tourists. Boggs lived in a large Victorian house on a dead-end street around the corner from the old Havenhurst Inn.

Vince answered Chet's knock, giving the three of them a friendly smile.

"Nice to see you again," he said to Frank and Joe. "How's it going, Chet?"

"Okay, I guess," Chet replied. "But I don't have much to do since Goodrich threw us out of Trusty."

"Not me," Vince said. "I've been busy figuring out new ways to support my lab work."

He ushered them into the house and led them from a large entry foyer into a wide hall that swept to the back of the house. From it, another, narrower

91

hall branched off at a right angle. "Here we go," Vince said. "This is my wing of the house."

"You have your own wing?" Joe asked in disbelief. "Isn't that kind of unusual?"

"Not for me," replied Boggs with a wide grin. "When I got interested in science, my parents thought I ought to have my own space to pursue my interests. They're both college professors, so they understand the importance of *individual* study." His grin widened. "But between you and me, I think they didn't want to know what I was up to. Which is probably just as well."

Frank and Joe looked at each other. What did Boggs mean by that?

"I mean, it's not as if I was going to blow up the house or anything," he added as they passed a huge bedroom on the left with a greenhouse-style sunroof. A large telescope was aimed at the expanse of glass. Next they went through a fire-resistant doorway into another hallway, which was faced in glazed bricks like a school corridor.

"And here's my lab," Vince said. "I've taken every precaution to minimize damage in case one of my experiments goes wrong."

"Wow!" Chet said. "What a setup!"

Vince smiled and said, "Now you can see why I had to work so hard at Trusty Home Products. We're not rich. The house has been in the family for generations. Both my parents have to work really hard just so they can keep it going.

"What are you guys interested in seeing?" Vince

continued without stopping for air. "I hear you're real science buffs yourselves, that you built your own telescope when you were nine or ten years old. Wait until you see mine. I've developed this great feature that lets me look at the same star or planet at two different magnifications at the same time.

"But tell me about *your* telescope," he went on. "I'd like to hear all about it."

"Well, there's not really much to tell," Frank said in a modest voice. "We were pretty young when we built it." He flashed Chet a look behind Vince's back. Chet shrugged helplessly. He had obviously exaggerated the Hardys' scientific background in order to avoid any suspicion about why they were coming along with him to visit. Frank wondered if it might have been better just to tell Vince the truth.

Frank cleared his throat. "We'd really like to see and hear about all *your* experiments today," he said to Vince, "and then another time you can see our lab."

"Okay," Vince said, grinning. "You're on."

He steered them around the well-equipped lab, showing them various experiments he was doing with mice and fish. As he talked, Joe looked at Frank and rolled his eyes. Frank stifled a yawn. Vince was really into his work, and it was obvious he knew what he was talking about, but it just wasn't the kind of stuff Frank and Joe were interested in. And none of it had anything to do with the case.

"Now, take a look at this. I've actually perfected

93

an invention that I think will revolutionize every-day life," Vince said, leading them to a corner of the lab. "It's a remote-controlled time-delay de-vice."

Frank and Joe jerked up their heads. Suddenly they were both wide-awake.

"That's very interesting," Frank said, trying to sound casual. "How does it work?"

"Well, say you get up in the morning and you forget to turn on the coffee maker. You're getting ready for your shower and you don't want to wait until you come out to start the coffee. You press a code into a wall device like a receiverless tele-phone. If you're not home, you just dial a pocket-sized encoder. The device is hooked up to appliances in the house. You can make them do what you want, *when* you want."

Frank looked thoughtful. "That's a great device. It could really give you control over your life. It takes up where programmed appliances and micro-waves leave off." He rubbed his chin. "I suppose it has its downside, though. For instance, it could be used to control other people's lives, too, couldn't it?"

"Well, sure," Vince said with a slight frown. "But who would care about turning on somebody's else's coffee maker or washing machine?"

"No, I wasn't thinking about those things," Frank said slowly. "I suppose it could be hooked up to things like, uh, explosives and set them off from a distance."

Joe stared at his brother. He'd been thinking of the device in terms of the driverless truck of the night before, not in connection with explosives. But it made perfect sense.

Vince turned slightly pale. "I guess so. It never occurred to me before."

Frank continued in a casual voice, "I was just thinking, in a case like, say, that Trusty Home Products explosion, if the circumstances were right, everything could be in place, and you could just phone a number and set off the explosion."

"If you had a telephone or a relay receiver on the site," Vince said reluctantly.

"Oh, it can work on a relay device, too?" asked Frank innocently. "So you could just plant receivers anywhere with your code or maybe even run them on a battery."

Vince's face went from pale to red. "Look," he said. "I don't know why you want to talk about the Trusty explosion. I thought you were here because you're into science."

"We *are,*" Frank said. "I was just setting up a hypothetical situation."

"You're acting as if you think *I* had something to do with the explosion," Vince said angrily.

"Cool down," Joe said. "No one was suggesting that you had anything to do with it. It just probably came to Frank's mind because it happened so recently and, after all, we were there."

Vince looked at the Hardys, but there was nothing in Frank or Joe's expression to suggest that either of them was anything but mildly interested in the remote-control device.

"Why don't we take a look at that telescope now?" suggested Frank.

"All right," Vince said with a nod. "But first I have to make a phone call. It'll only take a few minutes. I hope you don't mind."

"That's okay," Joe said. "We'll just take a look at your notes on fish breeding." He picked up a loose-leaf notebook to show Vince he was serious.

As soon as Vince was gone, Joe put down the notebook. "How did you connect Boggs's remote-control device with the explosion?" he asked his brother.

"I don't know," admitted Frank. "All of a sudden it seemed to make sense. By using the remote-control device, whoever programmed the explosion could have been miles away when it happened. All that person would have needed was previous access to the Trusty warehouse."

"Everybody involved with this case had that access," Joe said.

"True," Frank said. "But not all of them had access to a device like this."

"Do you think Boggs was the one who aimed that truck at you last night?" asked Chet.

Frank shrugged. "Well, he's the most likely suspect."

"I definitely think we ought to look for a link between Boggs and the explosion," Joe said. "When Goodrich made Vince stop seeing Denise, that could have given him a motive—revenge. And he certainly had the know-how. Let's see if we can pump him about Denise when he gets back."

"Good idea," said Frank. He bit his lip and thought for a minute. "He and Goodrich obviously hate each other. That fight Sunday night was definitely not faked."

"You've got my word on *that*," Chet put in.

"Maybe he's been blackmailing Goodrich, too," said Joe. "Like our friend Alison Rosedale."

"Good point. But if Goodrich could pin the explosion on Boggs, why would he go after Quayle?"

"That's a good point, too," Joe said. "What do you think, Chet?"

"I think I need some lunch," Chet answered.

Frank and Joe laughed, and the tension eased. Just then, Vince came back into the room. "I had to call long-distance to Florida about some fish tank materials. This was the only time the dealer was in the store. Sorry I was gone so long," he said. "How about some lunch? My folks left some good sandwich fixings in the refrigerator, and there's most of a watermelon, too."

"Sounds great," Frank said with a smile.

At lunch Frank, Joe, and Chet casually steered the conversation in the direction of Denise Goodrich. Vince wasn't too eager to talk about Denise. "It's over," was all he would say, adding, "the whole Trusty experience is history as far as I'm concerned."

After lunch, Frank, Joe, and Chet got up to leave.

"Thanks for showing us your lab and everything," Frank said to Vince. "You'll have to come see our lab soon."

"Terrific!" Vince said with enthusiasm. "I'll look forward to that."

"You know, some of Boggs's lab equipment looked pretty expensive," Joe said, when he, Frank, and Chet were back in the van. "How is he able to afford all that stuff?"

"Maybe he's blackmailing Goodrich as we said before," suggested Frank.

Frank drove the van out of the village of Havenhurst and past a large open field that separated it from the next town.

Suddenly Chet said, "Do you guys hear that? That ticking sound? It's coming from somewhere back here. At first I thought maybe something was just loose and bumping, but it's definitely a ticking."

Frank slammed on the brakes and pulled the van over to the shoulder of the road. They all leaped out.

But the ticking only got louder. It had to be coming from somewhere outside the van! But where?

Frank bent down and looked underneath the van. There was nothing attached under the chassis. He got up, walked to the back of the van, and looked at the tail pipe. Attached to it was a small time-device, ticking away. And the clock had ticked off all but two minutes!

Desperately Frank reached for his Swiss army knife and worked at cutting the cables by which the device was hooked to the van. The device came free, and he immediately positioned himself as if he were throwing a long pass. He heaved the bomb a couple of hundred feet into the open field.

"Duck!" he shouted.

10 The Aftermath

Frank, Joe, and Chet hid behind the van and covered their heads as the bomb went off with a deafening noise.

When they lifted their heads, all they could see was a thick cloud of smoke.

"Well, what do you have to say?" Frank asked. "Boggs is your friend."

"Hey, don't look at me, guys," Chet replied. "Remember, I was in the van, too!"

Cautiously, the three of them walked over to the field to inspect the impact. The explosion had left a large hole and an even larger circle of scorched and smoke-blackened grass and weeds.

"I just realized something," Joe said. "The carton of Splode-All—it's still in the van. We could have been blown away without a trace!"

"Well, we can be thankful for two things, then,"

Frank said lightly, trying to ease the tension. "We're still here, and *here* isn't Pine Beach. We can report what happened to the police."

"Are we still in Havenhurst, or is this Little Harbor?" asked Joe, looking around for a sign that might tell them where they were.

"Probably Havenhurst," Frank said. "We passed the police station on our way to Boggs's house."

The Hardys and Chet got into the van and headed back toward Havenhurst village.

"So much for Boggs's phony phone call to Florida," Joe said.

"He might have rigged up that thing while he was out of the room," Chet said. He shook his head. "I don't want to believe it, I really don't."

"It's the only possible explanation, Chet," Frank said. "Who else knew we were going over to his house?"

"Nobody except Iola and Callie," replied Joe. "Not even Aunt Gertrude knew where we were going."

"Could somebody have followed us?" asked Chet. "Or maybe somebody was driving by and saw the van."

"Boggs lives on a dead-end, remember?" Frank said.

"Oh," was all Chet could manage. He had a pained look on his face.

When the three of them got to the Havenhurst police station, they approached the desk sergeant and told him what had happened.

"Do you have any idea who might have done this?" asked the desk sergeant, whose name was Potts.

"Well, we're not sure," Frank said cautiously. "We were visiting a guy named Vince Boggs at his house in Havenhurst from about ten-thirty until just about five minutes before we discovered the bomb."

"What about this Boggs fellow? Do you know him well?"

"No," Frank said, "this is only the second time my brother and I have met him. But Chet here has known him about six weeks. They both worked for the same company. Boggs did leave the room for about fifteen minutes to make a phone call. I suppose he could have planted the bomb during that time."

"What company did you work for?" Sergeant Potts asked Chet.

"Trusty Home Products Company," Chet told him.

The sergeant looked thoughtful. "This wouldn't have anything to do with the bomb that went off at the Trusty warehouse Saturday night, would it?" he asked.

"We think it does," Frank said. "In fact, my brother and I—and Chet, too—have been looking into that."

"What do you mean 'looking into'?" said the sergeant. "Are you detectives?"

102

"Yes, sir, we are," answered Frank.

Something in the sergeant's manner made Frank go ahead and tell him what they knew about the strange goings-on at Trusty from beginning to end.

Sergeant Potts listened carefully, and when Frank had finished, he sat for a minute in thought. Then he said, "If Prescott isn't involved in this mess, then he's sure doing a half-baked job. They'd have my hide if I conducted an investigation the way he's doing it."

The sergeant paused a minute, then said, "Listen, I have a friend over in Pine Beach, the sergeant who works nights—*really* works nights. His name is Bill Clement. I want you to go see him. He'll be coming on duty soon. I'll give him a call if you like. He'll do anything he can to help you guys."

"Thanks, Sergeant," Frank said. "We've met Sergeant Clement once before—the night of the Trusty explosion. But we weren't sure if we could trust him or not."

"It's a big relief to know we can," added Joe.

"We'll run a check on Boggs," Sergeant Potts said as they were leaving. "Good luck. Keep in touch, and keep out of trouble."

"We will, sir," promised Frank.

When they were outside, Chet said, "That's a good guy."

"I bet he's a good cop, too," Joe said. "Not like our friend Prescott."

"Look," Frank said as they got into the van, "it's

been a long day—and we still have to talk to Iola and Callie to see what they've found out—but I think we owe it to Andy and his mother to let them know how things are progressing. Let's stop over there on the way home."

Joe and Chet both nodded in agreement. Then Joe asked, "Are we going to tell Andy that we found his signature on that invoice?"

"I think we should," replied Frank.

"From what we know now about the smuggling operation, that signature could have been forged."

"What if it wasn't?"

"We have to find that out," replied Frank. "But at this point, I can't believe Andy is involved."

When they got to Pine Beach and turned into the Quayles' block, they suddenly spotted the Quayles' white sedan ahead of them. Andy was driving, and Mrs. Quayle was beside him. At the stoplight, Andy saw them in the rearview mirror and waved. They followed him and pulled into the driveway behind the sedan.

Frank, Joe, and Chet jumped out of the van and approached the car. They could see that the backseat was filled with bags of groceries. "Here, let us help you with these," Joe said. "We have lots of news, and the sooner we get you unloaded, the sooner we can tell you."

The Hardys, Chet, and Andy began to carry the groceries up to the house.

"I'll be there in a second," Mrs. Quayle called

out as she slid across the seat to the driver's side. "I just want to get the car in the garage."

Reaching out of the window, she inserted a key into the automatic garage opener. She turned the cylinder, but the garage door didn't go up. It tore loose with a roar of explosives.

11 The Tip-off

The Hardys, Chet, and Andy dropped to the ground. Frank looked up and saw Mrs. Quayle scrambling out of the car.

"Get down!" he shouted. "We don't know yet if there's going to be another explosion!"

Mrs. Quayle fell to her knees. Crouching low, Frank, Joe, Chet, and Andy crept quickly away from the house.

"Are you four all right?" Mrs. Quayle asked anxiously.

"We're fine, Mom," Andy said.

"But I'm not so sure about the house."

They looked toward the house to see what kind of exterior damage there was.

The glass in the kitchen door had been blown out along with the frame. The clapboard around the blown-out frame showed some powder burns. The metal garage door had been cleanly torn off.

"It looks to me like the bomb was planted in the garage," Frank said. "What do you keep in there?"

"I've been using the garage to store my Trusty products," replied Andy. "I was planning to return everything to the company sometime this week."

"Well, we'd better not go in till we have the place checked out," Frank said. "There might be another device on a delay ready to go off. We don't want to be near the house if that happens."

Mrs. Quayle shook her head. "I just don't know how we're going to afford the repairs," she said, tears beginning to form in her eyes.

Andy put his arm around his mother. "Come and sit in the car, Mom," he said gently. "And don't worry. We'll work something out." He guided her toward the car and sat her down in the passenger seat.

A few neighbors who had heard the blast came up to her to see if she was okay. Joe asked one of the neighbors if he could use her phone to call the police.

"I got Clement," he said when he returned from making the call. "He said he'd be right over."

Sergeant Clement was as good as his word. He arrived a few minutes later accompanied by a police officer.

"You two guys keep showing up wherever there's fireworks," Clement kidded. "Guess you can't wait till the Fourth of July comes around again. It's only another fifty weeks away."

"I hope you don't think we had anything to do with all these explosions," Joe said indignantly.

"Don't worry," Clement said in a reassuring voice. "I talked to Sergeant Potts and he told me the whole story. I've known Potts a long time. He's an excellent judge of character."

Sergeant Clement and the officer left them and went to check out the scene of the explosion. A little while later, Clement returned. "My guess," he said, "is that this explosion, like that explosion over at Trusty, was a scare tactic. In both cases, the damage is fairly minimal."

"What about the bomb in our van?" Joe said challengingly.

"Now, that's a different story altogether," said Clement.

"You were on duty Saturday night, the night of the Trusty explosion, weren't you?" Frank asked.

"Yes, I was," Clement answered.

"Then why did Sergeant Prescott answer the call?" Frank asked.

"He radioed in, said he happened to be riding by when he heard the call, and told me he would answer it. Later, he radioed the station again and asked me to come out and take your statements."

"Did you know he was in his squad car, and in uniform?" Frank asked.

"No, I didn't," Clement said. "I thought he just

heard it on his CB. He made his report, processed all the paperwork, and told me he wanted to handle the case. I really haven't given it much thought since—until Potts called today and told me your story. And right now, I'd like to hear it again—from *you*."

Frank and Joe went over all the details of the case from the beginning, and they showed Clement the box of Splode-All and the pictures they had taken of the late-night delivery to the warehouse. Chet, who had heard the story before, walked off to talk to Mrs. Quayle. Andy stayed with the Hardys.

"All this sounds and looks pretty convincing to me," said the sergeant. "I can't believe Prescott thought he could get rid of you so easily."

"Well, we didn't show him the pictures from the warehouse," Frank said. "Remember, it was the phone call of his we overheard that led us there."

"But now we have a problem," Sergeant Clement told them. "I can't just take the Quayle case away from Prescott. And he can't get wind that I'm butting in, either. He's been sergeant for ten years, and I've been sergeant for barely ten months. Get the picture? But I'll do what I can."

"What about Chief Rudin?" Frank asked. "He's going to have to be involved, isn't he?"

Clement nodded. "He won't be the easiest person to convince. He trusts Prescott completely. And the chief won't be back from vacation until next week, so I can't tackle him before then, anyway."

"But you'll investigate the Trusty explosion and Goodrich's operation," Joe pressed. "Andy's trial is probably going to come up soon."

Sergeant Clement again said he'd do what he could. Then he told the Quayles that it was safe to go into the house. He and the officer got into their squad car and drove away.

Before the Hardys and Chet left, Frank told Andy about the signature on the invoice he had found.

"I do remember signing some blank invoices for Del Carson," Andy told them. "It was one day when he was out sick. I didn't think anything of it at the time. He sent a message through the receptionist, asking me to do it." Andy suddenly turned pale. "Did those invoices have something to do with the smuggling operation?"

Frank nodded. "I think they were Goodrich and Carson's way of keeping track of the shipments. But that's not all."

"Don't tell me, let me guess," Andy said, his voice beginning to rise. "If anything went wrong, they planned to use my signature as proof that I was working the operation." He looked at Frank, then at Joe. "Those creeps," he said hotly. "You've got to stop them before they totally ruin my life!"

"We will," Joe said firmly. "That's a promise."

After the Hardys and Chet said goodbye to the Quayles, they headed back toward Bayport and Chet's house. They were looking forward to hearing Iola and Callie's rundown of their morning at Alison Rosedale's house.

When they got to Chet's house, they found that Iola and Callie had sent out for pizzas.

"These look great," Chet said as he helped himself to a large slice of double-cheese pizza. He bit into it and sighed contentedly. "This tastes even better than it looks," he said.

While they were eating, Frank filled in Iola and Callie on the events of the day, ending with Sergeant Clement's promise to help them with their investigation.

When he had finished, Callie put down her napkin.

"Now it's our turn," she said. "The afternoon was truly amazing—just to see Alison Rosedale in action is something. She's an incredible dynamo. Once she gets going, she becomes more enthusiastic and more energetic as she goes along. And she kind of sneaks up on you. Before you know it, you're excited, too. That kind of persuasion can be dangerous when it comes to dipping into your pocketbook to buy cosmetics. Luckily we held her off.

"Anyway, after the demo was over, Alison served a buffet lunch. She was the perfect hostess, chatting with everybody, making sure we all had enough to eat. We couldn't get two minutes' worth of conversation with her. However, we did talk to her best friend, Laurel, and the subject of boyfriends came up. We told her that you were our regular dates, and then Laurel happened to mention the name of Alison's boyfriend. You'll never guess who it is—Del Carson, the Trusty warehouse foreman!''

"Carson!" exclaimed Joe.

"Wait, there's more," Iola said. "I happened to notice a shiny new baby grand piano by the window. When I pointed it out, Laurel said it had been a gift from an old family friend. That friend just happens to be a sergeant on the Pine Beach police force."

"Did she tell you the sergeant's name?" asked Frank.

"I asked her if it was Prescott," Callie said. "She said it was."

Frank and Joe stared at Callie and Iola. "You two are amazing, really amazing. That was great detective work," Frank told them, shaking his head slowly.

"Thanks," Callie said with a grin.

"Let's see how Alison figures in the setup," said Frank. He thought for a minute. Then he said, "Okay, tell me what you think about this theory: Carson either tells Alison about the operation, or she gets suspicious because of all his night work and finds out herself somehow. She goes to Goodrich to demand a piece of the action. He says no. So she gets her family friend—Sergeant Prescott—to put the squeeze on him. Make sense?"

"Maybe Alison and Carson set the Trusty explosion," suggested Joe.

112

"Wait a minute," Callie said. "We forgot to mention something—Alison was at the Iron Tiger concert Saturday night with Carson."

"Now I know why her car looked so familiar to you at the police station," Frank said to Callie. "It was the car that almost hit us after the concert."

"But how could they have set the explosion?" asked Iola.

"Easy. The way they were speeding, they could have beaten us to the Trusty plant. Or they could have used a time-delay device. Maybe Boggs supplied them with it." He shook his head. "But, somehow, I can't see Boggs letting someone like Alison use his precious invention."

"What about Prescott?" Joe asked suddenly. "Couldn't he have set the explosion? Remember what Sergeant Clement said, that Prescott told him he happened to be riding by."

"Right," Frank said. "That would explain why he was in the neighborhood. He knew he'd hear the call on his radio. His uniform and squad car would be a perfect cover."

"How do we prove all this?" asked Chet.

"That's going to take some time to work out," Joe said. "But we'll do it."

"Not if somebody blows you up first," Chet pointed out.

"And speaking of getting blown up," Callie said. "Do you still think it was Boggs who planted the bomb on the van?"

"Well, who else knew we were going to his house?" said Frank.

All of a sudden, Iola gasped. "Oh, no!" she said. "I almost got you killed."

"What!" exclaimed Joe.

"When we got to Alison's, she asked us how you were doing. I mentioned where you had gone . . ." She stopped and stared at the Hardys and Chet. "I can't believe I did that," she added in a horrified voice.

Frank thought for a minute. "Was Alison on the phone while you were there?" he asked.

Iola nodded her head yes. "She got a call," she said, "and it must have been a long one because she was out in the kitchen for at least fifteen minutes." She shook her head. "I didn't think anything of it at the time. I just never made the connection."

"Look, you couldn't have known what was going to happen," Frank said reassuringly. "Anyway, because of that bomb, we got Sergeant Clement on our side."

Iola shook her head. "I'm sorry, guys. Really sorry."

"Forget it," Joe said. "It's over."

"You know what?" Chet said. "I think we could all use some R and R right now. What about going to Emerson's Pier to hear some music?"

"That sounds like a great idea," Joe said.

The others agreed. They quickly cleared away the pizza boxes and cleaned up the kitchen. Then they piled into Chet's car and headed for the beach.

Emerson's Pier was a beachfront restaurant that featured local rock and jazz groups. It was a popular spot, especially with teens because only soft drinks were served.

Chet managed to find a parking space in the lot of the marina next to the restaurant.

"Oh, great," Joe said as they approached the restaurant. "There's a line as long as the equator."

"Be patient," Frank said. "Anyway, it looks like it's moving quickly."

Frank was right. After about five minutes, the Hardys, Chet, and the girls made it to the entrance. The entrance opened onto a dining room. Beyond that was an outside deck overlooking the water.

Suddenly Frank grabbed his brother's arm. "Look who's out on the deck!" he exclaimed.

Joe and the others looked toward the deck. Seated at a table next to the railing were Del Carson and Alison Rosedale.

"I'd really like to know what they're talking about," Frank said. Then he added, "That deck is set on a dune that slopes down to the beach. Carson and Alison are sitting right over that dune. Let's see if we can hide there and overhear their conversation."

"Right," Joe said, nodding. "Let's go."

"We'll get a table," Chet said.

"Good luck," Callie called out as the Hardys hurried out of the restaurant.

Frank and Joe sprinted around the side of the restaurant to the deck, positioning themselves on the dune just under Alison and Carson's table. The roaring of the surf and the clanking of dishes made it difficult to hear, but fortunately Carson and Alison both had voices that carried.

"Will you stop being mad at me?" Carson said in an angry voice.

"Why should I?"

"Look, all I said was I didn't want any part of your little extortion scheme."

"The trouble with you, Del, is that you're just not ambitious."

"That's not ambitious—that's criminal!" hissed Carson.

Alison gave a nasty laugh. "And I suppose that what you're doing when you deliver those goods isn't criminal? You just don't have the guts to stand up to Goodrich and show him what you're worth."

"Listen, Alison, just because I didn't want to spend the best years of my life in jail for trying to blow away two kids, I'm not weak."

"If you get caught, you'll go to jail anyhow."

"I'm getting out. I'm telling Goodrich I'm quitting."

"You're not serious, are you?" Alison sounded worried.

"Well, I'm thinking about it. Besides, you don't need me. You've got Prescott to do your dirty work. You can just sit back and clean up."

"But what about us?" said Alison, almost pleading.

"We can still be friends without being partners," Carson said hesitantly.

There was silence for a few moments. Then Alison said, "I want to go home now, Del. This conversation isn't getting us anywhere."

The Hardys heard the sound of chairs scraping across the wooden deck.

Suddenly a solid object fell into the beach grass right next to Frank and Joe.

"Oh, no!" Alison exclaimed. "My purse!"

"Take it easy," Carson said. "I'll get it."

The Hardys saw Carson easing his body between two railings. In another minute he would be dropping onto the dune. Right on top of Frank and Joe!

12 A Change of Heart

Without stopping to think, Frank and Joe sprinted down to the beach and ran along the water's edge until they'd gone past the restaurant. Then they headed back up to the street.

"I hope he didn't see us," Joe gasped.

Frank swallowed hard, then he shook his head. "It's a dark night," he said, between gulps of air. "No moon."

When they had caught their breath, the brothers made their way back to the restaurant. They were about to enter it when they saw Alison and Del Carson approach the door. Frank and Joe dropped back into the shadows. They watched Alison and Carson head across the street and get into Alison's sports car.

The Hardys entered the restaurant and found Chet, Callie, and Iola sitting at a table close to the bandstand.

"What's Alison's address?" asked Frank.

Callie told him, including the best way to get there.

"Chet, can we borrow your car for a little while?" asked Frank.

"Sure," replied Chet, digging into his pocket for the keys. "What's up?"

"Tell you later," Frank called as he headed for the door. Joe followed, looking puzzled.

"It has to be Prescott," Frank said when they were in Chet's car. "He's Alison's legman. We need to find a way of trapping him—and Goodrich and Alison and whoever else is involved—and we have to act fast, before anybody gets hurt."

"Or killed," added Joe. "But would you mind telling me where we're going now?"

"We've got to get Carson to help us," said Frank, heading the car toward Pine Beach. "You heard him tonight. I think we can persuade him to, in exchange for a lighter sentence."

"Do you think Sergeant Clement will go for it?" Joe asked.

"Unless he has anything better," replied Frank. "I'm just hoping Carson stays at Alison's long enough for us to get there."

The traffic was light, but it still took the Hardys a little under half an hour to get to Alison's. They parked down the block from her house.

"There's a beat-up sedan in her driveway," Joe said, craning his neck. "Let's hope it belongs to Carson."

119

They watched the house for about fifteen minutes. Then the front door opened and out came Del Carson. He got into the sedan and drove away. Frank followed him.

"What if Carson's got a gun?" said Joe.

"I'm taking a gamble he doesn't," Frank replied. "Remember, we're dealing with a young guy who's gone along with his boss for the money. He's not a killer—he refused to place the bomb on our van."

They followed Carson to a garden-apartment development at the other end of Pine Beach. Frank and Joe waited until he entered a ground-floor unit. Then they stepped to the door and rang the bell. There was no answer.

Joe knocked on the door.

"Mr. Carson, are you in there?" he called.

"Yeah. All right, I'm coming."

Frank and Joe heard the chain lock being unhooked. Then Carson opened the door. He had unbuttoned his shirt, and he had a towel around his neck.

"What are you doing here? Get lost!"

Carson tried to slam the door on them, but Joe had put his foot in the doorway.

"We need to talk to you, Carson. But you need to talk to us more," said Frank.

"If you don't get out of here, I'll . . ."

"You'll what?" Joe said. "Call the cops?"

Carson looked at them for a moment without saying anything.

"All right, what do you pests want?" he said finally.

"We need your help, and you need ours," said Frank.

"I don't know what you're talking about," Carson said, slipping the chain on the door, apparently having decided it was useless to try to get Joe's foot out of the way.

"We know what's going on at the Trusty warehouse," said Joe.

"What do you mean?" Carson challenged.

"Come on, Carson, we know all about your part in Goodrich's smuggling sideline. We know about Maury and Benson, what those shipments are . . . should I keep going?" Frank said. "Now, are you going to let us in?"

They heard the door being unchained, and then it opened.

"You've got five minutes," Carson said evenly.

When Frank and Joe had come in and were sitting on a sofa facing Carson, he said, "Why did you come to me and not the police? Oh, I get it—you want a cut."

"No, it's nothing like that," Frank said. "When we heard you tell Alison tonight at Emerson's Pier that you wanted to get out of the operation, we thought we'd take a chance and talk to you first."

"You heard us? How?"

"We hid on the dune next to the deck where you were sitting," said Joe.

121

"How come I didn't see you when I climbed down there to get Alison's purse?" Carson asked angrily. "Oh well, it doesn't matter. Go on."

"I know we took a big chance coming here," Frank said. "But we're sure Andy Quayle had nothing to do with the explosion at Trusty last Saturday night, and we want to get him off."

"Look, guys, I had nothing to do with that explosion," Carson said. "You've got to believe me."

"We'd like to believe you," Frank said, "but the way things are, we figure you and Alison could have set it up."

Carson shook his head several times. "I didn't do it! And neither did Alison. First of all, she's too smart to get involved in that kind of hands-on operation. And secondly, we were together that night."

Joe nodded. "We know that, too," he said.

"Look, we'll take your word for it for now," Frank said to Carson. "But what we really need to know is are you going to help or not?"

"Okay, okay," Carson said with a sigh. "But what do I get out of it?" he added.

"Probably a lighter sentence," Frank said. "But you'll have to work that out with Sergeant Clement. Should I call him or not?"

"Call him," Carson said quietly. Then he stared at Frank. "Wait a minute. How come you're calling

Clement and not Prescott? I thought he was in charge of this case."

"We think it's a very good possibility that it was Prescott who set the explosion."

Carson just sat there as Frank made the call to Sergeant Clement.

The sergeant arrived ten minutes later, accompanied by the same police officer Frank and Joe had seen at the Quayles' house earlier. Clement listened to Carson's confession, then he said, "I think we're going to have to catch Maury and Benson in the act. I'll call the Coast Guard and set it up. Carson, I'm leaving Officer Meyers here. As of now, you're in protective custody." To the Hardys he said, "I'll call you tomorrow morning and let you in on the plan."

Frank and Joe walked out with Sergeant Clement. As he was getting into his car he said, "By the way, Sergeant Potts had a little chat with your friend, Vince Boggs. He admitted he made a phone call—to Sergeant Prescott. Seems he'd sold Prescott a copy of his remote-control device. Prescott gave him some story about wanting the device for the police department. Anyway, after your conversation with Boggs, it dawned on him that maybe Prescott wasn't using the device for peaceful purposes."

"Thanks, Sergeant," Frank said. "That clears Boggs."

After Clement had left, Joe said, "So Prescott planted that bomb in our van."

"Right," Frank said. "My guess is that after Boggs called Prescott, Prescott phoned Alison. She told him to do it."

"Like he does all her dirty work," Joe said.

"Come on," Frank said. "Let's get back to Emerson's Pier before Chet starts worrying that someone's tried to blow up *his* car this time!"

The next morning, Sergeant Clement called the Hardys to tell them the plan to stop the smuggling operation.

"It'll take two nights," he told Frank. "Tonight and tomorrow. Tonight we nail Maury and Benson; tomorrow, Goodrich. And I want you and your brother with me both nights."

That evening, Frank, Joe, and the sergeant sat in an unmarked police car in the diner parking lot. At the warehouse, Carson loaded the Trusty truck with the cartons containing Splode-All. He and Maury drove to Near Isle as usual for their meeting with Benson. The unmarked police car followed them.

The Hardys and Clement got out of the car and walked down the lane. They kept out of sight and waited.

Soon they heard the faint sound of a motorboat slowly approaching shore. The noise got louder, then cut off completely. About ten minutes later, they heard the sound of a helicopter. Cautiously, they moved forward. When they got close enough, they saw a Coast Guard chopper land on the shore. Two officers got out. Carson, Maury, and Benson started to run back toward the truck, but they were stopped by the Hardys and Clement.

The two Coast Guard officers strode up to them. Clement introduced himself and showed them his badge.

"Right, Sergeant," said one of the officers. "We'll take charge of these two now." He and the other officer firmly guided Maury and Benson toward the chopper.

"You should have seen Maury and Benson's faces when that chopper came toward us," Carson told them. "They looked like they wished they'd never gotten involved in this whole setup."

"They'll have a lot of time to think about that where they're going," commented Sergeant Clement.

The sergeant drove the Hardys and Carson to the police station. Frank and Joe had left their van parked nearby. "Is it okay if we drive Carson home?" Frank asked the sergeant.

Clement nodded. "I think that would be okay. Officer Meyers will be along in about ten minutes."

Frank aimed the van toward Carson's house. As he slowed down for a red light he pulled up alongside a familiar-looking car. His mind was on the evening's activities and didn't register right away whose car it was. So it wasn't until after he'd stared for several seconds through the window of the tan sports car at Sergeant Prescott's profile that Frank jerked his head toward Carson and yelled, "Get down!"

13 An Easy Solution

Fortunately, Prescott was looking straight ahead. When the light changed, he pulled away without a glance in their direction.

Half jokingly Joe asked, "Should we tail him?"

"Everything's already in place," Frank answered. "Let's not blow it by changing gears."

The next morning, the Hardys spoke to Clement, who ran over the details of the plan to trap Goodrich and Prescott. That night there was supposed to be another shipment from the warehouse. Carson would try to convince Goodrich that the shipment should go on as planned, even though Maury and Benson had been nailed. He was sure Goodrich would agree. Carson would also suggest that Goodrich get Prescott up to the complex to demand an explanation about why he'd let Clement get involved. Carson would be wearing a wire, and Clement hoped he'd be able to get Prescott to confess to the Trusty explosion, among other things.

If the plan worked, the case would be wrapped up, and Andy Quayle would be in the clear.

Frank and Joe planned to be on the scene, but waiting with Clement a safe distance away.

At six that night, the phone rang. Frank answered it.

"This is Carson," said the voice on the other end of the line. "Goodrich just called. He's biting. He was all upset. Said that Clement called him and wants to meet him at the warehouse at seven-thirty —with a search warrant. He said I'd better get over there immediately and help him get those cartons of explosives out of there."

"Did he say anything about Prescott?" Frank asked.

"Yes. He said Prescott would be there. Goodrich is furious with him for letting the case slip out of his hands. Goodrich can't figure out how it happened, and I'm sure that bothers him. Most likely he doesn't know how to handle things. And he likes to be in control."

"Okay," Frank said. "And after you stop for Alison, don't race her sports car up there. Take your time." As part of the plan, Carson, reluctantly, had arranged a date with Alison. Once they were on their way, he'd tell her he had to stop at the warehouse to help Goodrich with something for a few minutes.

128

"Good luck," Frank said.

"You, too," said Carson.

Frank and Joe had arranged to meet Clement and Officer Meyers in the diner parking lot. By the time Frank parked their van it was six-forty-five. There was no sign of Clement or Meyers.

"Let's go up to the warehouse," suggested Joe. "Maybe Clement and Meyers decided to go directly there."

They crossed the road and headed up the driveway. Goodrich's sedan and Alison's red sports car were parked in adjoining spaces in the Trusty parking field. But Clement's squad car was nowhere to be seen.

"What if Goodrich finishes moving the explosives out of the warehouse and onto the truck before Clement gets here?" Joe said in a worried voice. "And where's Prescott?"

Frank bit his lip. "I'm going back to the diner and call the station," he said.

The officer Frank spoke to assured him that Clement and Meyers had left over half an hour earlier. He said he'd try to radio their car and get back to the Hardys as soon as possible. Frank gave him the number of the diner.

"Nobody's picking up," the officer said when he called a few minutes later. "Are you sure they aren't there? Maybe they went around the back way."

"No," Frank said. "We would have seen them at

some point. There's no way they could have *come* from the back. There's only woods back there—no roads for half a mile."

"Well, sit tight," said the officer. "I'll send a patrol car out to look for them."

"Right, thanks," Frank said, replacing the receiver with a bang.

He ran back across the road and up the driveway to where Joe was waiting. He quickly filled his brother in on his conversation with the police officer. Then he said, "I think we should go into the warehouse. That will stall them at least. Goodrich will have to drop whatever he's doing and deal with us."

"How will we explain what we're doing there?" asked Joe.

"Does it matter?" Frank said. "He isn't going to ask. He's just going to put two and two together and figure we're snooping around again."

"Okay," said Joe, nodding. "I'm with you. Let's go."

They continued up the driveway to the loading dock. The truck was outside, half loaded, but no one was with it. So they went through the door and into the warehouse. From the main room they could hear loud voices coming from a small room off to the side.

"Move it, Carson!" Goodrich was shouting. "You, too, Alison."

"You know, I don't have to do any of this," Alison

130

said. "It's your headache. I'm being helpful out of the goodness of my heart."

"Yeah," Goodrich said. "Then maybe you'd like to tell Clement how you would gladly have made it your headache, too, only I wouldn't let you blackmail me. Now, if you don't want your boyfriend to go to prison, you'd better get in gear."

Just then, Frank and Joe stepped into the room.

"Oh, great!" Goodrich said. "Now I have the two junior detectives on my case. I tell Prescott to get them off my back, but they keep turning up like bad pennies."

Goodrich pulled a pistol out of his jacket pocket and pointed it at the Hardys. Then he said to Carson, "Since we've been such successful business associates, I'm going to ask your help in arranging a little accident. We'll have to do it quickly and without any error."

"Now, look, Mr. Goodrich," Carson said in a desperate voice. "It's one thing to help you transport those explosives on company trucks. But it's another to actually mess with people."

"What about when you helped your girlfriend here set that explosion Saturday night?" Goodrich's voice rose until he was almost shouting. "You were messing with *me*!"

"You have the wrong guy, Mr. Goodrich," Carson replied. "Do you think I'd have been so eager to fix the damage if I'd caused it? And another thing. When Alison found out I was helping you with your little smuggling sideline, she wanted me to squeeze you for some more money, but I wouldn't go along with that. I just couldn't. So she got somebody else to help her."

Goodrich's eyes suddenly lit up. "Prescott?" he said. "So that's how he found out. That creep. He rigged that explosion! No wonder he got here so fast that night. And the next day he asked for more money. He called it protection money. But I didn't know it was to protect myself against him!"

"He's an old family friend," Alison said. "Naturally I turned to him for help."

"All I can say is so much the worse for him," Goodrich continued. "Prescott was always an honest, underpaid cop. Until he joined my club. If I weren't so mad at him, I'd have to respect him for being so clever."

Goodrich paused a minute. Then he said, half to himself, "I'll have to deal with Prescott later, but I might as well get rid of the rest of you now."

He sounded serious. Frank decided to stall by keeping him talking about himself, which he obviously liked to do.

"Was this worth it?" Frank asked. "Didn't you already have enough money from your business?"

Goodrich looked at Frank and gave a short laugh. "Do you think I could live the way I do from the soap business? I put a lot of hours into this and built it into something, but it isn't enough. I like to live well, but I can't do that *and* put away money in case Trusty goes downhill. What would I do then? I've always done a little something on the side, to sock away money, but nothing has paid as well as transporting Splode-All.

"I don't know who I get it from, and I don't care," continued Goodrich. "I don't know who winds up with it, and I don't care about that, either. And I don't intend to let any of you stop me."

Waving the gun to cover Alison, Carson, Frank and Joe, Goodrich said, "Now, move over there by those cartons along the wall."

They were herded so closely together that Alison's perfume, which had a strong scent of roses, clogged Joe's nose.

Goodrich reached carefully into his pants pocket and pulled out a book of matches. He tossed them to Alison. "You!" He pointed the pistol at her. "I want you to strike a match and throw it in the far corner. Then I want you to throw another one in that other corner. When we have a nice cozy blaze going, I'll leave you all, locking the door behind me.

"You, my dear Alison, will appear to have been the victim of your own little blackmail scheme. And you, Carson, will be presumed to have been her accomplice. And you Hardys—well, you will appear to have wandered into the wrong place at the wrong time."

Alison hesitated.

"Do it!" Goodrich shouted.

"Wait a minute," Frank said quickly. "You're forgetting one thing. Sergeant Clement will know

133

what happened. He won't let you get away with this."

"Judging from the lateness of the hour," Goodrich said, "I'd think that perhaps Sergeant Clement has been delayed—permanently! You see, when I called Prescott to tell him that Clement was coming, he said he'd try to persuade him not to come. I hope he was convincing."

Alison, seething with anger, said, "Tell me something, Bob. Have you given Prescott any payoff money?"

"Do you think my little operation would have run so smoothly if I hadn't?" Goodrich said.

"That rat!" Alison said. "I haven't seen a cent. And it was all my idea."

"Maybe he's been giving it to your mother to set up a trust fund for you," Goodrich said with a smirk.

"Don't make me laugh!" Alison said. "He's probably keeping it all for himself."

"I have to admit you tried," said Goodrich. "You're like me—you hate to lose."

"Why shouldn't I have gotten some of that money, too?" Alison fumed. "I worked hard enough around here. I'm entitled to some of the fringe benefits. If you think it's fun or easy giving those cosmetics demonstrations to a bunch of boring housewives, and to do all that driving and walking and delivering, you try it."

"Not likely," Goodrich said. "Now, let's get on with this." He held out the matches.

Alison reached out and took them.

"Light them and throw them!" Goodrich shouted.

Alison lit a match and threw it into the corner. A pile of rubbish immediately burst into flame. The flames shot upward, catching the end of a fabric wall hanging.

All of a sudden, the overpowering smell of Alison's perfume got to Joe. He let loose with a loud sneeze.

Goodrich was jolted out of his concentration, and Carson seized the moment to lift up a carton and throw it at him. Frank followed suit immediately, and he helped Carson tumble more cartons over in Goodrich's direction, knocking the gun from his hand and sending him sprawling.

The fire was spreading rapidly throughout the small office.

"Let's get out of here," Frank shouted. He, Joe, and Carson ran out of the warehouse and around to the front of the building toward the driveway. A huge clap of thunder sounded, then the skies opened up.

"Where's Alison?" Frank asked, looking back. But all he could see was a wall of pouring rain.

"She'll be okay," Carson said. "She'll get to her car on her own. She's been clever enough up till now. I don't think we want to wait to see if Goodrich gets up so we can stare down the barrel of his gun again."

They got to the van, jumped inside, and Frank

started the engine. The sudden downpour let up a little. As they were about to turn onto the road, Carson spotted Goodrich's car coming from the Trusty complex. It stopped at the end of the driveway.

"We didn't fix the louse good enough," Carson said. "We should have busted up his car, too. Now he's going to come after us."

"If only we knew where Sergeant Clement was," Joe said.

They turned onto the road. Frank drove quickly, hoping he could shake Goodrich. Joe looked into the side mirror and saw a familiar tan sports car following closely behind them.

"Oh, no!" he exclaimed. "Prescott's following us, too!"

14 Down the Barrel

Frank sped down the road, trying to lose Goodrich and Prescott. Suddenly, there was a loud thunderclap. Then torrents of rain began to swamp the van.

"Oh, great," Frank said. "As if we didn't have enough trouble!"

The windshield wipers were useless against the sheets of rain that pummeled the windows, and the roof sounded as if it were being assaulted by gravel.

"Joe, can you see if Prescott's still following us?" Frank asked.

Joe stuck his head out the window and looked back. "I can't see anything!" he shouted.

"We've got to try to make it to the Pine Beach police station," Frank said. "It's the only place I can think of where we'll be safe."

"What happens when Prescott comes?" said Joe.

"At least no one can shoot us in the police station and get away with it," said Frank.

As the Hardys drove down the rain-slick road, there was a sudden break in the downpour. Frank was able to pick up Prescott's car in the sideview mirror. It was about ten car-lengths back. Coming up quickly behind it was Goodrich's car.

There was still another couple of miles or so of woods and brush before they would get into downtown Pine Beach. As they rounded a curve, Frank had to brake in order to avoid skidding off the road. Prescott was forced to pass them to keep from a possible collision.

Prescott's sports car took the curve easily, but Goodrich went into a deep skid and careened across the road, off the opposite shoulder, and into some tall beach weeds.

"Step on it!" said Carson. "I think we can outrace Prescott."

Frank managed to pass Prescott just as the van hit another curve. This time Prescott pulled his easier-to-handle sports car in front of them and cut them off. In a split second Frank had to decide whether to rear-end Prescott's car or pull off the road. He tried to avoid Prescott. Attempting to pull around him on the slippery shoulder, Frank couldn't control the van. He ran into the ground alongside the shoulder and came to a halt, stuck fast in the mud.

Prescott ran up, his revolver flashing.

"All right, get out of there!" he ordered. Frank hesitated for a minute, then he opened the door

138

and slid out. Joe and Carson got out, too. Prescott motioned them into the woods.

"Sergeant Clement and Officer Meyers probably know what's happened by now. They'll be here any minute," Joe said.

Prescott laughed nastily. "That's what you think. Anyway, by the time *anybody* gets here, the three of you will be history. I think Goodrich, back there, already is. So I'm not worried. There won't be anything to connect me to any of this."

"What about Alison?" Carson said. "She knows you were double-crossing her!"

"I can handle her," Prescott said. "Now, march!"

He forced them deeper into the pines, where it was muddy and dark. The rain, coming down off the branches and the needles, soaked them.

"Won't it look strange when they find us dead with bullets from your service revolver in us?" said Frank.

"No," Prescott said, "because they won't. They'll find you dead with bullets from Sergeant Clement's service revolver in you. That's what I'm going to shoot you with."

Frank and Joe looked at each other. Before they could ask how Prescott came to have Clement's revolver, Prescott said, "Clement is such a dolt. He really thinks he's a good cop, just because they made him sergeant." He gave a snorting laugh. "You know, he and Meyers actually stopped when I flagged them down on their way to the warehouse."

"Where do you have him?" said Joe.

"I guess there's no harm in telling you, seeing as how you're not going to live to tell anyone else. I, uh, relieved them of their guns. Then I tied them up and drove their car off into the scrub a few hundred yards from here. As soon as you're dead, I'll release them. Without their guns of course. By the time the chief gets back and sorts out their story, I'll be out of the country."

Prescott smiled for a moment, as if pleased by his plan. Then he stopped smiling and said, "All of you, hands on top of your heads!"

Frank, Joe, and Carson did as they were told.

"Let's go just a little deeper into the woods," Prescott said.

As they trudged through the woods, Joe suddenly decided to try a stalling tactic. He stumbled and fell to the ground.

"Ow!" he shouted, as if in great pain. "I sprained my ankle." He tried to get up, but dropped to the ground again. "Hey!" he shouted. "I can't stand up."

"Where you're going you won't be doing much standing," Prescott said. "I can shoot you just as easily if you're sitting. Get ready!"

"You're the one who'd better get ready, Prescott!" called a voice behind them.

It was Goodrich, looking muddy and disheveled. He pointed his gun at Prescott. "Well, Mac," he said, "I guess we're at a standoff."

"Why don't you put that gun down," Prescott said in a reasonable voice. "We're still partners, aren't we? Even though I did set that little explosion at the warehouse."

"You creep," Goodrich said with a sneer. "Protection money. For you—the bomb expert. Now it's your turn to be scared. Drop your gun. Get over there with Carson and the hotshot detectives!"

Prescott shook his head. "Not a chance, Bob. If you want a Wild West shootout, that's what you're going to get."

Just then, the sound of a far-off gunshot pierced the air. Alarmed, Goodrich and Prescott whirled around.

"Now!" Frank shouted.

15 All Wrapped Up

Frank and Joe sprang at Prescott and forced him to the ground. Carson threw his large frame onto Goodrich in a wet, awkward tackle, wrestling him to the ground. Soon the three of them had both Goodrich and Prescott facedown in the mud. They forced the guns out of both men's hands. Carson handed Goodrich's gun to Frank.

Frank held the gun on Prescott and Goodrich as he led them back toward the road. Joe, holding the second gun, and Carson followed behind. Before they got to the road, two police officers—Sergeant Clement and Officer Meyers—ran up to them.

Prescott looked at them as if he were seeing a couple of ghosts.

"Are we glad to see you!" exclaimed Joe.

"How did you escape?" asked Frank.

Clement smiled. "I guess Sergeant Prescott here

was so crazy about getting our guns, he forgot to take our knives. It took us awhile to cut ourselves loose, but we managed to do it. Sorry it took us so long to track you guys down." He held out his hands for the guns. Frank and Joe gave them up gladly.

They all walked back to the road. Clement's squad car was parked on the shoulder. When they reached it, Prescott turned to Clement. "You won't be able to prove anything," he said sneeringly.

"Oh, yes, we will," Clement said with a smile. "Our friend Carson here has been wearing a wire all evening." He looked at Carson. "Is it still in place?"

"It was until I made that tackle on Goodrich before," Carson told the sergeant.

"Good," Clement said with a nod. "The entire evening's conversation is now on tape." He smiled at Prescott. "And by the way, Mac, the tape recorder is in the glove compartment of my squad car. Too bad you didn't know about it."

Prescott didn't say anything. He just looked down at the ground.

Clement and Meyers handcuffed Prescott and Goodrich, read them their rights, and pushed them into the backseat of the squad car.

At that moment another police car drove up, with two officers in it.

"These officers will take you home," Sergeant Clement told Frank and Joe. Turning to Carson, he said, "You can go home, too. But don't leave town. You're still facing a smuggling charge."

Frank and Joe asked to be taken back to their van. They spent the next hour digging it out of the mud.

When the van was finally free, they got inside and headed for home. There, Aunt Gertrude took one look at their tired faces and filthy clothes and ordered them upstairs.

"It's a good thing we have some of that new laundry detergent," she told them as they trudged upstairs. "Chet brought it over. It's called Trusty Brite."

Frank and Joe stopped in their tracks. They looked at each other and groaned.

The next day, Frank and Joe went down to the Pine Beach police station to make their statements. When they entered the squad room, Sergeant Clement was sitting at his desk, talking to Andy Quayle and his mother. Andy saw the Hardys and stood up to greet them.

"Sergeant Clement just told me I've been completely cleared," Andy told them. "I want to apologize to you guys for the way I acted at the beginning. And to thank you for everything you've done for me. Thank your friends for me, too."

"We will," Frank said. Then Mrs. Quayle added her thanks. "You'll have to come over for dinner soon," she told them. "After our house is repaired."

"How is that going?" Joe asked.

"Oh, fine," replied Mrs. Quayle. "Someone Andy knows from Trusty offered to do it for free."

"Who?" Frank asked curiously.

"Me," said a voice behind them. They turned around and saw Del Carson grinning at them.

Andy and Mrs. Quayle walked toward the front of the squad room, and the Hardys sat down at Sergeant Clement's desk.

Carson remained standing. "I figured I owed it to Andy after . . . well . . . after everything that happened," he said.

"We know about the invoices," Frank told him.

Carson nodded. "So does Sergeant Clement." He gave a shrug. "Anyway, I'll need something to do while my case is being prepared. I'm getting the public defender. I don't have my own lawyer."

"Listen," Frank said, "there's a friend of my dad's who we want you to talk with. He was going to represent Andy Quayle if he needed him."

"Really? You guys would do that for me?"

"Well, we couldn't have gotten to this point without you. And you did help save our lives," said Frank.

"Well," Carson said, "you guys helped save my life, too. I thought that made us even."

"Don't worry about it," Frank said. "Just do a good job on the Quayles' house. They've been through a lot."

"I'm sure he will," said Mrs. Quayle, coming up

to them. She smiled at Carson. "Are you ready to get started?" she asked him sweetly.

"Why do I get the feeling that Mrs. Quayle is a tougher lady than she seems sometimes?" asked Joe as the Quayles and Del Carson left the squad room.

Frank laughed.

"Okay, you two, let's have your formal statements," said Sergeant Clement.

When the Hardys had finished, Clement thanked them for their help. "Oh, by the way," he added, "the Havenhurst police picked up Alison Rosedale. She was pulled over for speeding and escorted here." Clement shook his head. "That girl is one cool cucumber. Do you know what she did while I was reading her her rights? She took a nail file out of her purse and began to file her nails!"

"What was she charged with?" Frank wanted to know.

"Attempted blackmail and a couple of misdemeanors," replied Clement.

The Hardys thanked Clement and left the station. They headed back to Bayport and Emerson's Pier, where they were meeting Callie, Iola, and Chet for lunch.

The three of them sat on the edge of their seats as Frank and Joe went over the events of the previous night.

"Incredible," Callie said, when Frank and Joe had finished. "Truly incredible."

Chet and Iola echoed Callie's sentiments.

"The whole setup got more complicated than Goodrich thought it would," Frank said. "He was letting the Splode-All be transported through his warehouse. Carson got involved by receiving and delivering.

"Carson, in turn, told Alison about his second 'job.' She immediately thought that he should be getting a bigger cut of the profits. She was very ambitious for him. When Carson didn't want to ask Goodrich for more money, Alison enlisted Prescott. She confided in him, and instead of turning Goodrich in, Prescott saw his own opportunity—to become a kind of 'business partner' to Goodrich. But he had no intention of sharing his cut with Alison. She was getting impatient. So she decided to try blackmailing Goodrich."

"But before that," Joe said, "Prescott decided he wanted even more money out of Goodrich, so he bought Boggs's remote-control device and, well, you know the rest."

"Did he set off *both* those explosions?" asked Iola. "And plant the bomb in your van?"

Frank nodded. "And he aimed that truck at us, too."

They all sat in silence for a few moments. Then Chet said, "Hey, now that this case is over, what about getting in some summer fun?"

"Great idea," Callie said. "What did you have in mind?"

"Well, we could go to the beach this afternoon.

Then, tonight, there's a concert at the Pine Beach Civic Center."

"I don't believe you." Callie stared at Chet.

"Don't you remember what happened the last time we went?" Iola added.

"Well, *I* remember," Joe said, a slow grin spreading over his face. "We had a blast!"

THE HARDY BOYS® SERIES
By Franklin W. Dixon

NANCY DREW® MYSTERY STORIES
By Carolyn Keene

	ORDER NO.	PRICE	QUANTITY
THE TRIPLE HOAX—#57	64278	$3.50	
THE FLYING SAUCER MYSTERY—#58	65796	$3.50	
THE SECRET IN THE OLD LACE—#59	63822	$3.50	
THE GREEK SYMBOL MYSTERY—#60	63891	$3.50	
THE SWAMI'S RING—#61	62467	$3.50	
THE KACHINA DOLL MYSTERY—#62	62474	$3.50	
THE TWIN DILEMMA—#63	62473	$3.50	
CAPTIVE WITNESS—#64	62469	$3.50	
MYSTERY OF THE WINGED LION—#65	62472	$3.50	
RACE AGAINST TIME—#66	62476	$3.50	
THE SINISTER OMEN—#67	62471	$3.50	
THE ELUSIVE HEIRESS—#68	62478	$3.50	
CLUE IN THE ANCIENT DISGUISE—#69	64279	$3.50	
THE BROKEN ANCHOR—#70	62481	$3.50	
THE SILVER COBWEB—#71	62470	$3.50	
THE HAUNTED CAROUSEL—#72	66227	$3.50	
ENEMY MATCH—#73	64283	$3.50	
MYSTERIOUS IMAGE—#74	64284	$3.50	
THE EMERALD-EYED CAT MYSTERY—#75	64282	$3.50	
THE ESKIMO'S SECRET—#76	62468	$3.50	
THE BLUEBEARD ROOM—#77	48743	$3.50	
THE PHANTOM OF VENICE—#78	49745	$3.50	
THE DOUBLE HORROR OF FENLEY PLACE—#79	64387	$3.50	
THE CASE OF THE DISAPPEARING DIAMONDS—#80	64896	$3.50	
MARDI GRAS MYSTERY—#81	64961	$3.50	
THE CLUE IN THE CAMERA—#82	64962	$3.50	
THE CASE OF THE VANISHING VEIL—#83	63413	$3.50	
THE JOKER'S REVENGE—#84	63426	$3.50	
NANCY DREW® GHOST STORIES—#1	46468	$3.50	
NANCY DREW® GHOST STORIES—#2	55070	$3.50	
NANCY DREW® AND THE HARDY BOYS® CAMP FIRE STORIES	50198	$3.50	
NANCY DREW® AND THE HARDY BOYS® SUPER SLEUTHS	43375	$3.50	
NANCY DREW® AND THE HARDY BOYS® SUPER SLEUTHS #2	50194	$3.50	

and don't forget...THE HARDY BOYS® Now available in paperback

POCKET BOOKS PRESENTS

MINSTREL BOOKS™

THE FUN BOOKS YOU WILL NOT WANT TO MISS!!